VOICES

Published by Morrigan Books

Östra Promenaden 43

602 29 Norrköping, Sweden

www.Morriganbooks.com

Editors: Mark S. Deniz & Amanda Pillar

ISBN 978-91-977605-0-8

Cover art by Reece Notley ©2008

First Published September 2008

VOICES

EDITED BY
MARK S. DENIZ & AMANDA PILLAR

MORRIGAN BOOKS

Available titles from Morrigan Books:

How To Make Monsters
By Gary Mcmahon

Grants Pass
Edited By Jennifer Brozek & Amanda Pillar

Dead Souls
Edited By Mark S. Deniz

The Phantom Queen Awakes
Edited By Mark S. Deniz & Amanda Pillar

Requiems For The Departed
Edited By Gerard Brennan & Mike Stone

Scenes From The Second Storey
Edited By Amanda Pillar & Pete Kempshall

Creeping In Reptile Flesh
By Robert Hood

DEDICATIONS

Amanda
For my mother,
Judi Jaensch.
My rock.

Mark
For my wife, Etina,
Without whom I would have no voice in this industry.

For Ross,
For giving me the idea and then letting me have it,
you are a gent in every sense of the word!

The Editors Would Like To Thank:
Reece Notley, Nyssa Pascoe, MG Ellington, Susie Hawes,
Andrew McKiernan, and all those who submitted to the anthology.

FOREWORD

Hotel bar: Conflux 4, Canberra, October 2007. Ross Temple and I were discussing his hotel room (as he was staying at the conference venue), and how its design was a little out of the ordinary. The talk began with how the structure of the room meant that a square bedside cabinet couldn't fit snugly into the corner of the room, and this lead to his idea that the hotel might not be all that it seemed.

The discussion moved forward, as I began to imagine the hotel built according to lay lines. This led to the idea of a witch staying in a hotel room, which inspired me to write. First though, I obtained full consent from Ross to steal his concept.

A couple of weeks later the room appeared too small; it seemed like the idea was much bigger than the room itself. Only one conclusion was forthcoming: the whole hotel was wrong, I needed more than one room. I needed an anthology — I needed other writers.

The decision made, I contacted Amanda Pillar (who had also been involved in the original discussion with Ross), and invited her to co-edit an anthology of original horror stories: stories that took place within a single hotel, but occupying different rooms within that structure.

We worked out our submission guidelines, which couldn't adequately convey what we wanted, but which I hoped would give the writers an idea of what we were searching for. We then sat down to wait for the hotel to be built, brick by rotten brick.

What you see inside these pages are stories that perfectly showcase my idea, born back in October last year. They detail the hotel that I and Amanda envisaged. A place that has a nasty history, a hotel filled with secrets, monsters, ghosts, witches, tragedy, loneliness, portals, murders, suicides, and all manner of dark subjects that transitory spaces capture so well — their claustrophobic otherness, a de-familiarisation apparent in each room.

Every room has a story to tell — the question is: can you bear to listen; can you bring yourself to hear the voices?

Mark S. Deniz & Amanda Pillar
September 2008

TABLE OF CONTENTS

PROLOGUE

1928

Ornate façades, miniscule pavements and the narrowness of the street made the hotel feel claustrophobic even from the outside. The front door was itself subtly foreboding — narrow, with stained-glass panels and an air of finality.

It said, *Abandon all hope, ye who enter here!*

"I don't like this!" Brighton Jones muttered grumpily — with luck, only to himself.

But Rosalyn heard. Grappling with both a portmanteau and an overstuffed travel-bag because the taxi-driver had refused to help, she bumped against him as she pushed past.

"Please don't start, dear."

Brighton sneezed. His head jerked forward. Letting the bags he was carrying drop, he rubbed his hand across his upper lip.

"For god's sake, use a hanky," Rosalyn snapped.

But by then his eyes had locked onto a dark-red stain on the sandstone of the first of three steps. He frowned as he knelt beside it.

"What are you doing now?" Rosalyn hovered over him.

Brighton's forefinger moved toward the stain. "I think this is blood," he whispered. His fingertip dipped in the wetness. He sniffed it. "Ewww! Smells like bird poop! Some pigeon must've been eating mulberries."

"Your nose is bleeding." Rosalyn straightened up and moved toward the door.

"Really?"

Blood decorated the side of his hand. Shoving the smaller of his bags under his arm and holding a handkerchief to his errant nostril he continued toward the hotel. Another red drop lay innocently on the top step and several more had reached the far side of the glass. How in god's name could he have sneezed blood there?

"Hurry up!" snapped Rosalyn.

Distracted by her tone, he trod right onto the trail of blood as he shoved himself through the door. His shiny leather shoe slid along the polished floorboards, forcing him to let go of the bags to retain his balance. They thudded and tumbled into the silent space. The door slammed with a loud clang. From various points across the lobby, scattered pairs of startled, curious or annoyed eyes turned in his direction. "Sorry," he muttered, self-consciously straightening his suit.

"Do be careful, *darling*," Rosalyn smiled, a viper in the curves of her lips.

"There was..." Brighton looked back as he gestured towards the scene of his social blunder, but he couldn't see any blood at all and decided not to continue the sentence.

"What?"

"Forget it!"

The anaemic, gaunt-faced man behind the registry desk radiated displeasure. It was a bad beginning. Brighton hung back in humble misery while Rosalyn settled the business side of things. He knew there'd be trouble once they got to their room. She was already in a foul mood, thanks to the sudden onset of "the curse", the rigours of the trip and the fact that he was an ongoing disappointment to her. His stint in the War — and a medal for surviving two years in the trenches — had only held sway over her affections for a short period after he returned.

Hopefully this establishment had an elevator that worked.

Then he noticed that there was blood — or what looked like blood — spattered on the registry counter, just under the overhang. He shuffled closer to get a good look, peering nervously.

"Stop that, Brighton!" Rosalyn mock-whispered. "You're embarrassing yourself."

He pointed toward the wood panelling (but it was darker now, obscuring what he'd seen). "There was rather a lot of blood on—"

"No, Brighton!"

He snapped his mouth shut.

Rosalyn leaned close to him so that he could smell her familiar perfume. It was an expensive brand, and quite attractive, but today it gave off a hint of sourness. "Dreams are dreams, Brighton. They don't belong in the waking world."

He frowned, wondering what she meant. "I know, dear, but—"

"No!"

A porter took her bags from her and led them toward the lift. Blood lay in sporadic curlicues along their path. When Brighton ventured to ask if she could see anything on the floor, the dark satanic warning that emanated from her face shut him up before he'd finished.

Waiting for the elevator, Brighton couldn't stop his mind from returning to the escalating bloodiness. Whenever he started seeing things that Rosalyn didn't, it inevitably caused trouble, which they'd come on vacation to avoid. Of course, it didn't help that when his attention was caught by the clunk of the elevator's arrival, the first thing he noticed was the thick red liquid that leaked out from under the doors.

"I don't like this," he whispered.

The elevator doors clanged open; the carriage shuddered uncertainly. "Wait!" he said, not looking at what was inside. "I want to go up the stairs. Ros, I think we should go up the stairs."

"Brighton!" she growled.

At first it was the vast splashes of blood — blood that dripped from the lift car roof, runnelled down the polished walls, gathered in puddles on the floor — that drew his attention. When neither Rosalyn nor the porter reacted, however, he assumed they couldn't see it — that it wasn't really there — and closed his eyes. He waited in the dark for a moment, feeling the ominous trembling in his muscles grow, then let the world in again, hoping the blood would have disappeared.

But this time he registered the elevator attendant. The figure standing at the control panel was dressed in the same uniform as the porter, but his clothes hung loosely on his skeletal form. The bones of his face were barely hidden under a veneer of pale skin, and his eyes were dark, almost absent. He stared directly at

Brighton as though he could see into his thoughts.

"We should go up the stairs," Brighton insisted.

The porter studied him blankly. Rosalyn grabbed Brighton's arm and dragged him into the car. "Don't be absurd, dear," she growled. "It's four floors up."

He didn't have time to resist. In an instant he was inside the elevator and the attendant shut the metal concertina door. "Our bags?"

"The porter will follow. Be still."

With a clang, the outer doors shut on them.

Inscrutably, the porter watched the chrome indicator above the elevator door-panel move from G to 1 to 2 to 3. He didn't react went it ground to a halt halfway to 4. He merely blinked when a series of distant shrieks echoed down the elevator shaft. He started back as the vibrations from a louder thud reached his ears, as though something heavy had fallen from higher up. The indicator returned to 2 then to 1 then to G. But the doors didn't open.

Only when blood began oozing out from under the door panel did the porter call for the manager.

ILLUSIONS

SANCTUARY

ROOM 116

CAROLE JOHNSTONE

He wasn't coming. I had been so sure that he would, but now I knew that he wouldn't. It wasn't that he had contacted me to tell me so, though that was his usual modus operandi: a wheedling drawn-out excuse that neither of us believed, and then the angrily swift withdrawal that I always fell headlong into. This time it was more a feeling — or an absence of it. A knowing. He wasn't coming. And I don't think that I was ever sure that he was, not really. Optimism is rarely the possession of a positive outlook; it's born of desperation. For me, anyway.

As a hotel room, it wasn't particularly awe-inspiring, but then I suppose they rarely are. A carpeted space maybe ten feet by fifteen; two shades of beige bisected by a pink flowery border, magnolias maybe; a mock Edwardian carver chair more suited to a dining room, its stuffing yellow and almost wiry where it had fought its way through what might have been tired leather. Two mismatched wardrobes that were inordinately large for the room were split by an Art Deco-type standard lamp that I already knew didn't work. Either side of the Kingsize there were two bedside tables: 80s-era and doubtless flat-packed; upon one, the obligatory miniature kettle, sachets of sugar, coffee, tea and plastic-wrapped shortbread. I had investigated the ensuite upon arrival. For a person like me that's as important as checking out the view. Or the fire-exits.

The first day had been all but over the time I arrived. I was knackered; the long train journey had all but killed me, and what medication I had was already going to have to last too long. I'd ordered room service at about eleven pm, expecting to be palmed off by the offer of a leftover sandwich at best, but the voice at the other end of the cracking line had been more than accommodating: its timbre low-pitched and oddly androgynous, though benign with the promise of lasagne *and* some sort of steamed pudding, whose name I hadn't caught.

Of course I shouldn't have had the lasagne. Or most likely, the pudding. Any fool who had voluntarily discharged themselves from hospital following the worst relapse of a colitis that had already resulted in ten previous stays and two hasty bowel resections, should have known better than to even *sniff* a plate of cheesy pasta. Lactose is no more a friend to me than all night benders or Indian restaurants. Or long train journeys. Or cities. Or stress. I suspected that I could now probably add Dan's name to what, over the last five years had swiftly developed into a very involved list — though he likely came under a few headings already.

The weather was bad the following day. I sat on top of my starchy counterpane for most of it, looking out at the grey scudding sky and the sun that struggled behind it. I watched those dark clouds roll past my window, and as the gloomy afternoon wore on, I watched them return. They provided an airtight excuse for going nowhere that hardly needed the reinforcement of numerous toilet visits and appointments with my old friend, Mr Steroid Enema and his mistress Suppository.

Though it was my only real distraction, I could only stomach the portable Goodmans in small doses. There was no satellite (thank God for small mercies), but static, daytime telly — punctuated by inane adverts offering solace to viewers whose worst afflictions appeared to be bloated post-Christmas bellies and high car insurance premiums — was doing my soul as much good as Italian food and Dan's no-show. The first time I caught my own eye in the tarnished portrait mirror above the TV table, I flinched at the dead-eyed, slack-jawed, grey-faced apparition that blinked back. The second and third times, I just looked away a bit quicker.

That night, my belly rumbling and sore from lack of food as much as the day's exertions, I lay still on top of the bed's covers like an already dead person: arms folded on my chest, my index fingers resting against my collarbone, staring up at the ceiling with hard dry eyes. In the fading light, I thought I saw movement there

— or the suggestion of it: a fly or dust mote that you only managed to see once it had already gone from view.

I felt a sudden tightening in my chest that was not quite fear, though a real and present press at my throat threatened to rectify that in the instant before I realised that only my own fingers had crept up to my neck. The pulse there was ridiculously fast, and although I concentrated hard on my breathing, I still strained to see what I had seen on the ceiling. Nothing. Probably only artex. I was usually a big fan of artexed ceilings: their careless swirls and peaks calmed and hypnotised, while the smooth painted plaster that everyone else in the world seemed to favour left me queasy and reminded of the skin on cold custard.

❧

The nightmare was as chaotic and patternless as my ceiling: a derangement of images and bellowed threat that snuck in under the cover of gentle reminiscence. Lying on the top bunk in my childhood bedroom and reaching up to break off longer unchecked drips of artex; listening to the wind chime that was really just a tied together jumble of Dan's unwanted CDs on the balcony outside our flat; smelling the citrus of pink magnolias along the old railway behind Grandpa's allotment.

And then the whispers. The whispers that too swiftly became shouts and odious shuffles on the periphery of my vision. The ceiling that dropped inexorably down towards my face like some tired 80s adventure movie set in Egypt. The horrible drip drip drip of toxic chemicals into my body, pushed and checked by nurses who would not look at me because they had no eyes. No faces. The long clunking MRI tunnel that slowly swallowed me from the feet up: a cold and deafening crematory furnace. And then those awful screams.

When I awoke I think I screamed. In fact I know I did, because that ceiling — that moving, writhing ceiling — was already pressing hard on my nose and my chest. When I reared up from the bed, I fully expected to knock myself out on its sharp and malignant surface, but it had already begun retreating backward, *upward,* and its scuttling parasites had become little more than moving shadows that again I couldn't catch.

When nobody came at my scream, I stumbled out of bed, pushing up on a sash window until gusts of biting air lifted the hair from my skin, replacing bad chills for good. Crawling back to the bed, I drifted back into a blessedly dreamless sleep quickly, the shout of the wind reuniting me with a sense of space. And a peace of sorts.

In the morning I lay in bed too long, breathing long and sonorously through an open mouth, watching the reflected rain stipple against my ceiling. It wasn't artex after all; it was as smooth as a baby's bottom. Or a bowl of left custard. If the familiar rumble in my belly came as a surprise, then the roaring, griping, *clutching* agony that gripped it soon after terrified, and only once I had stumbled into the bathroom, voided what felt like every organ in my body, and spied all my nasty paraphernalia under the sink, did I remember who I was. *What* I was.

While suffering through my usual post-ablutions regime, I concentrated only upon building upon that memory. That this should be difficult at all both alarmed and shamed me. It was as if I were scuba diving — and right down, down at the silted bottom, where everything was muffled and muted and unhurried even although I was sprinting like mad inside my brain.

I remembered the hospital first, and then the pain of dropping ten pounds and shitting little else but blood the three weeks before it. And I remembered running from that hospital; running from the cold ministrations of its nurses and the solemn predictions of its doctors — running anywhere else but home. Lastly, I remembered my name. Any sense of achievement at this was somewhat diminished by the fact that the mere recollection of who I was should have been any exertion at all.

I glanced at the ring on my finger and the way the circular fluorescent caught it when I squinted. I found better solace in that than anything else, even if Dan's likely desertion should perhaps have depreciated its power. I was no longer trembling when I stepped back into the room, though I was still frightened enough, not only of my transient memory loss, but of what might have caused it — and of what might cause it again. More than that, I was afraid of my own apathy; a numb and lumbering passivity that I could no longer shake. I was completely alone. Though I suddenly felt far from it.

I stared at the phone for a long time before I picked it up and punched 0. Why, I couldn't have explained any more than any other thought I'd had since waking. I only knew for certain that I didn't want to speak to that strange and dilatory voice again. It felt like reaching out to pet a dog that had once before turned on me with frenzied eyes and biting teeth.

This time, I ordered dry Weetabix and filtered water: the panacea of the intestinally-challenged. This time, that peculiarly unaffected yet epicene voice seemed a little mocking; a little *too* knowing. And when I finally managed to get out my order (in as stilted a voice as its own), I could have sworn that it chuckled.

I didn't switch on the Goodmans all that day, though the queer lethargy that was not quite lethargy gradually faded as the afternoon wore on. On either side of the mirror above the dusty screen there were two surprisingly cared for prints that I watched on and off instead, while the rain battered against the windows and shrouded my pink and beige room in shadow. One was a bunch of folks sitting and dancing in the Paris sunshine. I recognised it from art history; it had likely saved me from a foundation repeat in the fifth year: Le Moulin de la Galette. And alongside it, a picture that I didn't like at all — in fact I might even have recoiled a little from it upon first glance.

In the foreground, a man and a woman were striding out of range; or rather he was striding and she meekly following. He was wearing a crown of leaves and a belted tunic reminiscent of Richard Burton in *Alexander the Great*, and carrying what I thought might have been a lyre. Behind them a dense, and it seemed to me very sterile forest, squatted in wreathed grey-green sunlight, exposing malevolent figures in hooded robes that I knew were watching the fleeing couple, though their bowed hoods pretended indifference as they huddled low to the silver-grey pond between. Even the sky: a bright and distant mauve that I felt certain was supposed to hint at freedom, the existence of better places — perhaps even the obligatory light at the end of the tunnel — had exactly the opposite effect on me. It made me shudder the longest.

At some point in the late afternoon, I forced myself to get close enough to look properly, spilling the bowl of old and scentless potpourri that sat next to the TV in the process. I pretended not to notice; the same went for my absurdly shaking hands. I was getting good at not noticing. There was a small laminated plaque tacked beneath the print, and in a typeface almost too flowery to read, I made out: *Orpheus leading Eurydice From the Underworld; Jean-Baptiste-Camille Corot.*

I started to feel sick, and then I got angry. What the hell was I doing here? Why had I come? The answer might have been in another spasm of my ulcerated, shrinking bowels, and at that moment I would likely have gladly swapped that anonymous room for an anonymous ward brimming with brilliantly disassociative consultants and indifferent nurses. Though ever having been anywhere else at all suddenly struck me as being a very long time ago. And the panicked moment passed as swiftly.

I spent too much of the day staring at that picture. And too much of what was left staring up at the horribly smooth ceiling, sensing flickers of movement underneath that were not completely there; still not enough to actually *see* — but close enough for jazz all the same. At some point I became aware that there was something watching me from the corner; standing close to the tweed patterned curtains that I had only half drawn. But not even when it started to whisper did I look.

Dinner arrived as the shadows in the corner lengthened, heralded by the now familiar single knock, though I could not this time recall having picked up *that* phone again to ask for it. That got the ever present chills on the back of my neck dancing faster. I got to the door as quickly as I could (uncomfortably reminded of Pavlov's dutiful little subjects as I did it), but when I pushed open the door, only a tray of what might have been risotto greeted me.

I looked up and down the empty corridor and at the closed door opposite. The rusted 6 of the 16 had worked its way loose and hung down in a drunken 9. I realised that I couldn't remember what number I was — if I'd ever known — but I also realised that I didn't want to go into the corridor to find out. Lifting my dinner from the floor with only a slight wince at my poor bruised insides, I retreated backward and closed the door with relief.

I managed to eat most of the eggy rice (it was kedgeree not risotto), perched uncomfortably on the edge of the bed that faced away from the figure close to the curtains that had started up its inane whispering again, and the brittle *infected* picture that was the very antithesis of the golden smiling shine of its partner. The ceiling still pressed too low above me, and this was harder to ignore, though I carried on trying to.

After eating, I busied myself with making coffee, another recent addition to my *To be Indulged at your own Peril* list. There was a bible stashed behind the kettle tray: a black leather-bound Gideon that I considered picking up but didn't. A thought suddenly struck me as the low rumble of the kettle drowned out my companion's mutterings. One that found just as apt an association in the manner in which I took receipt of my food. You could *always* rely on there being a bible somewhere in your hotel room, even if it was stashed apologetically away at the back of a drawer. There was only one other kind of place that adhered to the same obligatory rule and it certainly wasn't a hospital — although God knew, there if nowhere else was where the need was likely the greatest.

Too soon it was night; too soon the high-dose steroids and anti-inflammatories kicked in, and my weary body gave up the fight, dragging me back to the bed and my corpse-like pose. But my mind came alive. In the dark, and in the shadows *outside* the dark, my mind came suddenly alive where it had slept soundly all day. And it kicked and it screamed. Louder than the soporous and drowsy breaths that rose and fell within my chest; louder than the resumed movie creak of the dropping ceiling and whatever creatures writhed and skittered under its jagged surface. Louder even than that *something* in the corner next to the half-drawn curtains — no, closer now — I could hear its manic yet torpid mutterings much closer now. Perhaps as close as the Goodmans. Or the picture. When the timbre of its shuffling changed; when it encountered the scattered potpourri in dragging snaps and rustles, I realised that it was closer yet. Probably close enough to touch.

And still I felt I was struggling too deep under water. Only there was no flash of sunlight on the surface; no bright mauve sky beyond the trees. No citrus scent of pink marigolds or tinny chimes of metallic plastic. There was only this creeping, spreading return to paralysis, and the smell of pond weed and brittle winter forest. And the sense that I'd left it all too late. I was already lost inside that forest; I had already forged too far ahead before recognising what the acceptance of my fate had really meant for me. What it meant to me *here.* A loss of identity. Imprisonment. And maybe something far, far worse.

I stumbled from the bed, a high scream providing the only energy that I could draw upon. A juddering ataxia had gripped my legs, and I careered towards the door, my hands outstretched in the dark like a zombie in drink. I probably screamed again when my forgotten companion snaked vine-like arms around my waist, my torso. Its muttered breath was wet earth and sweet rot. Its grip held me fast in a straightjacket as it propelled me with it. When I *definitely* tried to scream again, something — a root maybe, damp and barbed with scratching fibrils — shot around my cheek toward my mouth, and I swiftly closed it shut without ever having uttered another sound.

We didn't make it as far as the door, not that I had ever suspected that we would. Another nasty, creaking whisper at my right ear precipitated a more recognisable click, but even then I still recoiled from the sudden return of light. My eyes adjusted horribly fast. They were mere inches from whom I had guessed was Orpheus, his gaze not the heroic impassivity that I had imagined while his face had still been turned away from view. Now he stared out of the frame with eyes that were haunted and frantic — and full of terrible realisation.

My captor muttered more nonsense into my ear. It trickled deep in icy rivulets. In the reflection of the light above the bed, he was an indistinct head atop a narrow, ductile neck that poked out from behind like an offshoot of my own. I probably tried to scream again. I could feel my memories, my thoughts, and God forgive me, even my darkest intentions since that last prognosis, draining from me like blood. I could feel all that I had ever been disappearing into that hellish purple sky above the trees. A brittle dazzling edge of steel that was more than terror — now far *beyond* terror, saw me stagger against the Goodmans as my captor snaked more vines around my cheeks, my temples, forcing my gaze from the fleeing Orpheus and Eurydice, and onto the dreadful huddled spectres beyond them.

Close up, their furtive scrutiny was more obvious, more triumphant. I could see the teeth that hid within their low hoods — their filed and crowded teeth that grinned at our doomed escape. *You can't get out,* those mouths muttered too close to my ear. *You're too deep in the forest now; you're too deep in with us.*

And God help me if there weren't more than just the five that I had already seen reflected in the murky grey-silver pond at the picture's centre. God help me if there weren't *dozens* rising up from the wet, green floor; from behind skeletal trees; from the misty reeds of the water. If they had been there before I had not seen them. I hadn't looked hard enough. Or perhaps I had. Perhaps I had seen them just as well as I had seen everything else in this room that had never been a room; this escape that had never been any kind of sanctuary at all.

I had one more thought; just the one before that life ended and this endless perdition began. Before yellow-green decay and shadowed woodland rushed in. And it was perhaps something that should also have occurred to me long before. Long before I had checked in *or* out. Courage is often in acceptance and rarely in flight. And more often still, the loss of memory is not an affliction. It is the only offer of escape that any of us will ever get.

CAROLE JOHNSTONE

BIOGRAPHY:

Carole Johnstone was born and raised in a small town east of Glasgow. At 20, she moved to England, where she worked as a radiographer and then a medical physicist.

A relative newcomer to the world of published fiction, she was recently featured in Black Static Magazine, and is due to appear in the anthologies: *In Bad Dreams Vol.2*, Eneit Press; *Scenes from the Second Storey* and *Voices*, Morrígan Books, and *In the Footsteps of Gilgamesh*, Gilgamesh Press.

As well as looking for an agent/publisher for her first novel, she is presently involved in her first collaborative project: co-writing a story within a collection of shorts and novellas.

Her website can be found at www.carolejohnstone.com

AFTERWORD:

Hotel Rooms. There's something about hotel rooms. A familiarity that is as soulless as it is anonymous.

You show me a person who says that they like spending time alone in a hotel room, and I'll show you a liar. Quite apart from the obvious connotations: those long endless corridors and distant banging doors, those queer noises coming from the room next door...there is also the question of who was there before you. What part of themselves did they leave behind?

Speaking from personal experience, hotel rooms for the solitary traveller are a necessary evil: four too-close walls and a mirror in which you might not want to study yourself too closely.

In *Sanctuary*, I wanted to create a character who imagined that she was running from something far worse; a character for whom the ubiquitous hotel room was just that: a sanctuary. And I wanted badly to prove her wrong.

The picture that features in the story is one that has long affected me. The depiction of the Underworld as a wraithlike forest hiding hooded and watchful spectres is sinister enough, even before you start to notice all of the others crouching in the shadows. And you have to look hard. I don't think I've counted the same number twice.

As to the conclusion of *Sanctuary*, the choice is yours to make. Maybe she was only crazy; maybe it was the picture. And maybe it was just what gets left behind.

My money is on the hotel room, but I've clearly got issues.

THE MIRROR

ROOM 105

K. V. TAYLOR

The music got louder and louder every time Max glanced toward the mirror.

There was something sprawling and epic about it, like a never-ending circus parade. Only there were no elephants, monkeys, or clowns, none of the things he remembered from Ringling Bros. These images were dimmer, half-melted, pulled apart pieces of things he couldn't grasp. Shadows and shapes roiling, bubbling and spitting and moving to a pointlessly syncopated march.

It wasn't real, not in any sense but the most existential. Max wasn't crazy. He knew *that* much.

Nevertheless, it was getting louder. The tiny bones in his ear seemed to rattle, which shouldn't be happening if it wasn't real.

And god, it made him tired.

"Go back to bed," Luca warned, muffled by the pillow.

The sound of his voice, half-asleep, made goosebumps break out all over Max's skin. Small hairs stood upright, made him itch and tingle.

By the time the feeling faded, Luca was breathing regularly again — the deep, soft breath of someone sleeping peacefully.

Max turned his eyes back to the mirror. The blackness of the room took shape in its surface, the stripe pattern of the wallpaper appearing out of the dark, the shabby pale curtains and Luca, a smallish mound of blankets on the far side of the bed.

The problem with the music was the dissonance. It never resolved, never gave him a chance to *understand* the things it was showing him.

It had been five days. And it was still getting louder.

∾

His back ached, his arse having sunken long ago into the

crevasse between mattress and headboard. Luca was out, finding something to eat. Max supposed that was good, since really he ought to be hungry.

The music wasn't so bad when it was light out, but Max still hadn't slept since they'd left home. He hadn't slept for days before that, either.

Music was not natural. He'd had a music teacher in fifth grade; she'd tried to tell him it was the language of the cosmos, the perfect mathematical expression of reality. But all she ever heard was the plodding regularity of Bach. *This* music spoke of impossibility. It was like having his head picked apart by vultures while he sat and watched.

And those fuckers in the mirror were all to blame. For everything.

I haven't slept for days.

❧

The crisp sound of the door clicking back into place, and Max's heart leapt into his throat. His back went rigid, he winced in pain.

"We're running out of cash, but I haven't seen anything on the news. We might be in the clear."

We. Luca always said 'we', as if it had anything to do with him.

"Why are you doing that?" Luca asked.

Max looked up and saw Luca depositing a brown paper bag on the small table. It was dark already. Max hadn't noticed before, but maybe he'd had his eyes closed. It was getting harder to remember anything. But he still wasn't crazy, because he knew what was real.

"Max. Why?"

"What am I doing?"

Luca stared at him, a pair of glinting eyes from the shadows now. "You're tapping your finger against your leg."

Max realised that he was, in fact, tapping his finger against his leg, trying to decode the beat that tortured him. "I'm... trying to..."

"It's back," Luca said grimly. He shot a hateful look at the mirror.

Max shook his head. "No, I just… I just…"

He couldn't think of a good excuse, but he couldn't tell Luca. He'd be so disappointed.

Anyhow, there was nothing they could do. Even if they covered it, he'd still hear the music. They'd tried that last time. And breaking it was even worse…

"Are you hungry?"

Max nodded, felt something in his stomach that took him a good three seconds to figure out. It was relief, he realised.

He accepted a bag of Chee-tos and a Bud Light. Luca turned the television on, but Max tuned it out. He had to *listen* to the music, or it became *noise*.

Maybe that was why he was so tired; because it was so hard to *listen* to something that didn't make sense.

৽

Luca snored sometimes when he drank too much, and the noise made Max want to cry.

He watched Luca's face in the mirror, pale and thin and looking too old for his age. The music was as mercilessly irregular as ever, but slower, and it let a small portion of his mind stop searching for its pattern.

Long enough to consider his companion. Six days now, and no one had come looking for them. Maybe no one had noticed yet. Maybe—

I haven't slept for days.

Max noticed something twitching in the corner of the mirror. To his irritation, he realised it was his finger, tapping out some horrible syncopated rhythm that would never stop, and never form any recognizable thing.

Schizophrenics found patterns in what was unreal, and no patterns in what *was* real. Luca had told him that. But if he couldn't find a pattern in *this*, and it was *un*real, he definitely wasn't crazy.

Just tired.

He made his hand stop twitching, and his fingers started to ache. Luca sighed in his sleep, and Max shifted his gaze in the mirror to him. Luca's lips parted, moving now.

Moving with the music.

Max stopped breathing.

Yes. The time changed there and Luca's lips were following.

Max reached out to stop them in a desperate burst — the first time he'd moved anything but his fingers in hours. His arm ached, his lungs felt crushed.

The mirror went dark, all but Luca's face, which was deadly white. And his mouth, grey in the dark, curled into a sudden smile. Not Luca's smile though, something exaggerated and mocking. Too big for Luca's small, pointed face. Getting bigger, bigger, showing teeth, stretching lips, gums bleeding and the music was getting louder and louder and *laughing at him—*

"Max!"

Max cringed a little at the sound.

"Max, wake up!"

He wasn't asleep, though.

&

"What the fuck are you doing?"

He was… being shaken, apparently, by Luca.

Max pulled out of Luca's grip — and in the process realised that he had a grip on Luca as well. On his shoulder. And his fingers were sticky-wet.

"Did you have a nightmare?" Luca insisted, intense in the dark.

Max swallowed hard, eyed his friend carefully — face to face. Luca still looked pale, but his mouth was pinkish instead of that dead grey colour. And not twisted into a distended evil smile.

"I got scared," he said.

He couldn't tell Luca what he'd seen in the mirror. It would just make him worry more.

Maybe they could go home soon. It'd be okay if they could go home. He slept better there.

"You dug your claws into me." Luca relaxed visibly as he spoke. He swung his legs over the edge of the bed and stood, already moving toward the dark rectangle in the wallpaper that signified the bathroom door. "You looked seriously scared. Maybe we should find you some sleeping pills — they might get rid of the dreams."

"I haven't slept in days," Max muttered.

But Luca was flicking on the bathroom light, which caused bright yellow to overflow into the rest of the dingy hotel room.

Max wiped the blood off his fingers with the sheets and closed his eyes against the light.

And the mirror.

⁊

"Do you want to go outside?"

Max shook his head quickly, not wanting to speak if he didn't have to. He wished he could tell *Luca* to stop speaking — it was hard enough to listen to *them*, let alone him talking about nothing.

But he couldn't say that to Luca. If it weren't for him— ... *in days*.

"It's been a week since you've left the room. You probably don't realise, but the place smells like shit."

Max could hear the smile in Luca's voice, but he didn't look at him to see it. The thought of it made him cold.

He didn't smell anything, anyway. Heard things, saw things, but that was it.

The bed shifted — Luca's weight on the far corner. "And you look like shit, by the way."

The smile was gone, so Max lifted his eyes from the bedspread. The flash of the mirror caught his eye, his imagination, a great wave of atonal madness crashed over some obscure part of his brain.

He twitched slightly, and his eyes finally made it to Luca.

Luca's Adam's apple travelled down, then back up very slowly. "This is crazy," he said quietly.

"No," Max replied. The sound of his voice was shocking — gravelly and decaying. It bounced around inside his skull, added to the cacophony until he was able to sort it all out again, for one painstaking second. "I'm not crazy."

Luca's lips twitched slightly.

Max's back went rigid until he realised it wasn't a smile. It was the opposite.

Luca's eyes were wet now. He squeezed them shut, took a deep breath.

Max waited, something tearing at his insides that, for once, he knew was very real. But it was all he could do to keep the vultures in his head at bay. If he started crying too, it would be over.

❧

No, he'd been wrong.

Music *was* natural. He felt it now, felt it in the way it was unravelling him. His mind would never get used to it, he knew. He'd always be searching pointlessly, endlessly, for meaning where there was none. It was just chaos.

That was natural, wasn't it? Order was a human imposition on the universe. On music, even.

What he was hearing *was* real, just not in the way he'd expected. Dissonant strains in endless combinations — just when he ceased to find them dissonant anymore, they changed. He reeled.

He didn't even think he was tired anymore. He was discovering what it meant to exist; how could he be tired?

"Max."

Max inclined his head slightly, eyes fixed on the mirror.

"Last night, when you had that nightmare? When you scratched me?"

"Yeah," Max grunted. The music pounded suddenly — caused a small explosion of electricity to course down his spine.

"Was that how it was… when you did it?"

Max didn't know what he meant, so he didn't answer.

"When you… do you remember doing it?"

"I hadn't slept in days," he mumbled.

Luca's face looked odd in the mirror. Twisted up, lips pressed thin, eyes narrowed. Max recognized it vaguely as fear and worry.

"Maybe we were wrong," Luca suggested. "Maybe we should've gone to a doctor instead. You're getting worse."

"Better," Max corrected. He tried not to be angry at Luca for interrupting, for adding to the chaos. There was a symphony, but it wasn't Luca's fault he couldn't hear it.

℘

Parts of him wanted to move — like someone was poking bits of his brain with a galvanized needle, making him into some kind of Frankenstein. Only, *they* were doing it, and their noise, their music, was the needle. His fingers wouldn't stop twitching and his foot now did the same.

"No one knows it was us," Luca whispered in the dark.

Max saw him in the mirror, curled up on his side, facing the door.

"Me. It was me." He'd done it, Luca had only found him after, and tried to protect him from himself. But he'd been so tired. And the music did things to him — confused him, made him someone else.

"You, us, whatever at this point. No one knows. It'll be okay soon. We can go home."

"Okay."

Long moments passed; entropy on display in Max's head. He stared unblinking at the mirror, until every feature of the room revealed itself in it again. The striped wallpaper; the shabby curtains; Luca. Things he understood; things that weren't real.

A sudden movement distracted him, the noise to become overpowering for just a moment — a bedlam of sound, no one part distinguishable from the others. Luca had flipped onto his back, eyes closed, chest rising and falling.

The sound split open, black and harsh, and he found a thread again. It was insubstantial, slipping out of his grip as quickly as it had come.

Luca smiled in his sleep, in the mirror. Max watched, the noise rising and falling with maddening unpredictability, as the smile grew wider and wider. As if Luca knew.

And then it wasn't Luca's smile anymore. And there was a hole in not-Luca's chest, deep and black, that should not have been there. It split him open, defied his anatomy, and ignored his rib cage. He gaped, but not from his mouth. Gaped and mocked, and his foot began to twitch with the impossible rhythm flushing

33

through Max's brain.

Something inside the music laughed, and Max went rigid, his heart soaring and thudding with jarring regularity. The rush of blood in his ears had a pattern, and it brought tears to his eyes, blurred the vision in the mirror, the room around him, until it all melted into gray. The noise rushed up then, angry that regularity had intruded, maybe, and regained its place. Snatched him back and slammed forward, fever-pitched. He felt his body twitching, convulsing, following orders he'd never given. Violent, extreme, and accompanied by the icy sound of something shattering.

When he opened his eyes, his entire body ached with exhaustion. And there was something slick and dark on his hands. He looked around now, at the room. Luca was still beside him, on his back, but the black hole in him was real.

No. No, it was just something black on the sheets, down Luca's front. And he wasn't smiling, his mouth was just open. Like a silent scream in his sleep.

The noise ended abruptly. Max shivered once, and it was gone.

The emptiness made him cry with relief, blurring the vision of the oddly mangled body beside him. The thing that used to be Luca, but wasn't anymore.

It was just like last time.

But Luca said no one knew it was them. It was *him*.

He hadn't slept for days. They'd go home soon.

Pieces of mirror flickered all over the room; some of them streaked with black-red something. Max watched the biggest one he could find, until he finally heard a sound.

Quiet, eerily familiar chaos.

Max wiped his hands on the bed sheet and waited.

K.V. TAYLOR

BIOGRAPHY:

K.V. Taylor is a freelance editor and lover of dark fiction and fantasy. Originally from West Virginia, she currently lives in the D.C. Metro Area with her husband and mutant cat. This is her first publication.

AFTERWORD:

While in the middle of writing a paranormal horror story about mirrors, I started researching the effects of music on the brain and was inspired. The concepts in the current thought about tension and resolution, what we expect from a piece, and why we love the music we love, struck me as both fascinating and potentially horrifying. Unresolved chaos in music has been known to incite public riots, and that made me wonder what it could do over a long period of time, then, to a single person.

HIS ONLY COMPANY, THE WALLS

ROOM 126

BRAD C. HODSON

Hi! You've reached Julia's cell. Leave a message.

I think I lost you. My signal's weak out here. I was just calling to say I'm at the hotel and settling in. I bought a bottle of champagne, some French kind that I can't pronounce. The girl at the off licence recommended it. I saw a few nice restaurants on the way up that we could visit, too. We should celebrate, you and I. We've been waiting for this for far too long. If I hadn't…

Well, I don't guess that matters now. Hope not, anyway. I *have* been taking my pills. I hate the things, but I know you want me to take them, so…

Um, anyway, I'll keep an eye out for you. Try not to be too long. Call me.

Love you.

Hi! You've reached Julia's cell. Leave a message.

Hey. Me again. Where are you? Why aren't you returning my calls?

Ummm… just call me back, I guess. I love you.

Hi! You've reached Julia's cell. Leave a message.

Hey. Just checking in, seeing what your status is. About to go out and look for a pharmacy. These things go fast. Want me to pick up anything? Gimme a call.

Love you.

Did you call earlier? My battery died and I forgot to put my phone on the charger. It's charged now, so just call back. If you did. Earlier, I mean. Call either way. Please.

Voicemail again, huh?

I wish you would answer. My head's been itching. It's this horrible feeling inside my skull, like maggots are burrowing against the bone and trying to find a way out. I've scratched it until it bleeds, but nothing works.

If I scratch any harder I'm afraid I'll dig up long strips of flesh.

I'm being gross, aren't I? Sorry. It's just getting to me. This room. The itching. You not calling. I had that dream again, too. Is "dream" the right word? More like a memory, I guess. Where I came after you at your work. I shouldn't bring that up, I know. Is that why you aren't calling? I was hoping we had gotten past that by now.

Maybe this was too soon. Maybe I should have cancelled this whole trip. What do you think?

I love you.

Walls *can* talk, you know. Every time someone mutters "If these walls could talk..." they have no idea how close they are to one of the great secrets of the world. Most people have never been able to hear their walls, maybe because their walls have weak voices, or maybe they just don't have much to say. But if you spend enough time on the road bouncing around from hotel to hotel, you start to pick up on the subtle whispering that leaks through holes in rotting wallpaper and from behind tacky thrift store paintings of schooners at sea or atrocious farmhouses. It's like reading, really; until you learn how to listen it's just random humming, but once you do you can't turn it off.

I've been wasting away here waiting on you, my only company the walls. It took me a few days to puzzle out their language. I thought it was simply the hum of electronics or heating vents at first, but then I pressed my ear against the flowery wallpaper and heard your name. I wish they would shut the hell up; I don't believe a thing they're saying about you.

This room reminds me of that first weekend that we spent away together. Remember? We rented that convertible. Some kind of Chrysler, I think. "Seafoam Green" the brochure declared, with a CD player and cruise control. The sun blanketed us as we sped up the Pacific Coast Highway, a large mountain pressed against your side of the road and the long drop to the crashing surf below on mine. It was raining slightly, and you thought that was strange because of how sunny it was.

"The devil's beating his wife," I said.

You laughed and asked what the hell that meant. "I don't know," I said. "Just some odd Southern-ism my mom used to say whenever it rained while the sun was shining."

We had done the typical wine country tour that marked us as tourists, stopping at each winery just long enough to lose a little bit of our inhibitions before heading to the next. A far cry from the stinking flesh and acidic mouths that pressed against us at that punk show where we met.

What was that band called? I can't remember.

The hotel we stayed at that weekend was much like this one — the worst room in an otherwise decent place. The wallpaper was the same nicotine stained colour, and the windows were littered with the same dried out husks of flies that had somehow found their way into the room but never left.

What a horrible end for those things, being able to see the outside but not to reach it, pounding their heads against the window until they crushed their pathetic little insect skulls.

Not that any of that ugliness mattered to us. We never left the bed.

The couple in the room beside me reminds me of us. They fucked all night last night. I couldn't sleep a wink. Their grunts and ecstatic moans blasted through the flesh thin walls with such volume that I could have sworn at one point *I* was the one fucking. Even the air conditioner, one of those hotel standard issue models with a jet engine crammed inside of it, couldn't drown them out. I cranked the thing up all the way and buried myself inside my blankets, but even its colossal roar couldn't match Mr. and Mrs. Holmes next door. Eventually even the walls grew tired of them.

God, I wish you would hurry up and get here. Why aren't you—

BEEP!

I miss you. I'm sorry for… everything, ya know? Just… just call me back. Please? I love you.

Been staring out the window for so long that my eyes have gone weak. I keep tricking myself into thinking I see your car slowing at the traffic light, rainwater cascading from your roof and swirling around your tyres. I tick off the seconds (135 to be exact) that mark the duration of the red light. All you have to do is turn left when the light changes, pull into the car park and park below my room. 131, 132, 133— it'll change soon and you'll turn left.

The light changes and you drive straight, speeding off into the distance. As the taillights fade I remind myself that it wasn't really you, just an imposter, some vicious bastard masquerading as you.

The walls whisper amongst themselves, arguing over if it will ever be you. One wall thinks that you will come, but that you'll change your mind at the last minute and decide not to turn. That wall says you'll take the path all of the illusions of you have taken. The rest doubt that you're coming at all.

I tune them out. They're all wrong, aren't they? You'll be here soon.

My itch keeps getting worse, especially at night. I guess I've been scratching it in my sleep. There are little trails of blood on my pillow when I get up, and I can feel fresh scabs hiding under my hair. How do you stop an itch this bad?

The front desk clerk just came by. He wanted to know how long I was extending my stay. I had originally checked in for two days. I've been here for… God, has it been over a week already? I guess so. Kind of starting to feel like home a little. Well, not quite. Not without you. But close.

I told him "indefinitely" and gave him the MasterCard.

Room service came after that. Cheeseburger, fries, and a coke. I've been racking up quite a tab here; I haven't left the room in the past couple of days in case you call. My cell phone signal is a little weak out here, and I'm afraid if I drive down to one of these pitifully small neighbourhood markets I'd miss you.

I mean, miss your call. I already miss you.

Your phone's probably about to cut me off again. Please just call and let me know what's keeping you and when you'll—

BEEP!

I'm sorry I haven't called you in the past few days. The walls were telling me I shouldn't. They said I may be putting too much pressure on you. Am I? I usually don't believe them (they lie so much), but if I am then I'm sorry.

I've lost count of how long I've been here. They bring a credit card slip for me to sign with my lunch every day. I've been sleeping too much — twelve hours sometimes. It's just so damn hard to wake up, like I'm floating in the depths of some warm, comforting body of water, and to wake means breaking the surface and being subjected to the icy air above.

You're there also, when I sleep. Just dreams, I know, but still…

I've been doing aerobics. Sounds funny, doesn't it? At least I'm not wearing a leotard. It's just something to occupy my day and stay in shape while I wait. Plus it's the only daytime TV I can stomach. Have to be in good shape when you come, though, right? I have to be able to keep up.

I've also been catching up on my reading. I've already finished the actual books I brought (*The Stranger* and *Slaughterhouse Five*), and I've moved on to e-books. It's a little hard on the eyes staring at my laptop's monitor for so long, but it's either that or surfing junk sites.

I almost went for a walk today, but something kept me from it. Part of it was being afraid of missing your call, I guess, but there was something else. It's kind of hard to explain. It was like the idea of going outside filled my stomach with acid. I don't know why; maybe I've been inside these walls for too long. I'm sure that'll change when you get here.

Someone knocked on my door a couple of hours ago. I thought it was you and rushed to answer it, but no one was there. Whoever knocked was fast, I guess. I mean, I instantly opened it. They had knocked pretty damn hard, too, like they desperately needed something. Must have been kids.

Well, I'm going to go before your voicemail has a chance to cut me off again. Call me, okay? Please? This is killing me.

Where are you?

Hey. It's me. I just thought of something that tickled the old funny bone. Do you remember that night at your brother's birthday party? When me and your brother got into that fight? Your brother was saying that I was too poss—

Hold on.

...

Sorry. Someone was knocking at the door again. I wish I could catch whoever's doing it. I'd rip the little shit's throat open.

What was I saying before that? Fuck. I don't remember.

SHUT UP!

Sorry. Not you. The walls were — never mind. Never mind the walls. It's best to ignore them.

Are *you* ignoring *me*?

Sorry. Forget I said anything. Call me.

Hey. Me again. Of course. How are you? *Where* are you? You were supposed to be here sometime last month. I know you couldn't give me an exact date, but this is getting a little ridiculous. I wish you would at least just fucking call me. Why can't you just pick up the goddamn phone and...

Sorry! Sorry. I'm just stressed. I didn't sleep last night. That fucking kid pounded on my door every three or four hours. Of course he wasn't there by the time I got out of bed. I called the front desk, and they said they would look into it. Fat lot of good that will do.

The weather here is awful. It's been raining so much that the veil separating earth from the heavens must have ripped open. The wind rattles the windows so hard I'm surprised they haven't shaken free from their sills. The sky's the color of charcoal when it's turned to ash. Even if I wanted to leave the room I wouldn't in this kind of weather.

I've been watching the hotel across from mine. There's a girl there. A prostitute, I think. Maybe just the local slut, I don't know. There's always a different guy going in and out over there. In between them she likes to stand against the railing in front of her door and smoke. She's got this stringy blond hair, like she hasn't washed it in days, and she always wears this pink baby doll tee. Her limbs are little more than bone with skin stretched over them and a few bruises painted here and there. She saw me watching her earlier and winked at me. I shut the curtains.

Don't think I'm planning on going over there or anything. I'm just bored.

You know; if you get here before the weather—
THAT KID'S KNOCKING AGAIN!
I'll call you back!

Julia...
...
...fucking bitch...

I'm sorry about that last message. I'm just... you know... I'm sorry. I didn't mean it. I love you. Just please come. I'll make it up to you when you get here.

The knocking's gotten worse. I don't know how they get away with it, but they're doing it every couple of hours now. I tried leaving my door open to catch them, but I didn't like that. It didn't feel right, having that door open.

I tried asking the walls who it was, but they've grown strangely silent. Thank God for small favours, I guess.

I screamed at the kid, told him I would rip his goddamn tongue out and kick his guts until they were a bloody mush. I guess I went overboard. Someone called the front desk and the manager came to see me. He said that another outburst like that and they'd have to ask me to leave. I can't take that. I've been here for so long now. What would I do out there? I have to watch myself.

At least the kid stopped knocking. The walls have been whispering again, but very softly and only to each other. I can't make out what they're saying anymore.

Probably for the best.

I can hear him, shuffling up and down the hall, moving back and forth past my door. He's out there right now. I've been listening to him for the last hour, my head pressed against the door so hard I can see thousands of tiny little stars, an entire galaxy hidden inside my skull. The way his feet sound, it's like he's limping, or maybe pulling one useless foot behind him like a soldier dragging a corpse.

Who is he? What the hell does he want?

I keep putting my hand to the knob, thinking I'll swing it open fast enough to catch him. But I can't. I'm worried about who could be out there in that hall. Maybe I'm worried that no one will be there.

The walls only whisper when he's not around. When the shuffling stops, the walls talk amongst themselves. When he comes back, they go mute. Why? I tried asking them, but they're ignoring me now.

Jesus, I need you here. I need to get out of here, but I just can't. I can't.

Not without you.

That prostitute keeps watching me. I've got the curtains closed, but whenever I peek out from behind them she's there, just staring at my window. What's so goddamn interesting about me, huh?

The itching is unbearable. I scratched it hard enough today to pull a little hair out. Maybe there's some kind of lotion or—

Shit! He's outside my door again. I've gotta go. I don't want him to hear me.

He's calling now. I know it's him. For the past three nights, three calls a night. Midnight, two, and four. I called the front desk, but talking to them is like talking to the rain; the rain just keeps falling, heedless of how I beg.

The first two nights he didn't say anything. I yelled into the phone, but he wouldn't say a word. The last call, the one at four last night, he…

Ah, shit.

He asked about you. By name.

"Have you spoken to Julia?" The voice… Christ, it was strange. Listening to it made my skin feel like insects were crawling all over it, burrowing inside it, laying eggs in it. It was hollow and tinny, but low. Rumbling, like a hearse driving over gravel. It's the voice I imagine tombstones would use if they could speak.

And the way he said your name! He drew the syllables out, like he was tasting each one. It came out like "Jooool… yahhhhh…"

I hung up and took the phone off the hook.

What am I going to do? I can't leave; he's out there in the hall somewhere. If I stay here he'll come for me, I know he will. I managed to eavesdrop on the walls (they thought I was sleeping) and they said that he *was* coming for me. They sounded frightened.

For the love of God, please hurry. Please.

I'm so hungry. I haven't eaten since… I don't know… I'm afraid if I call room service that when they knock and I answer the door, *he* will be there.

He's probably there now.

I watched that prostitute again today. She had her door open and a pizza box on her bed. She was eating so slowly, grabbing a slice every half an hour or so, raising it to her mouth at the speed that leaves change colour, and chewing it with her mouth open. I could smell it; this had to be a trick of the mind. I mean, there's a pane of glass and a car park between us.

She saw me sometime after the third slice. God knows what I look like right now, with bald patches exposing bits of dry, scabbed over scalp. She must have thought I was salivating over her and not the pizza. She put it down and slid the strap of her shirt from one shoulder, revealing a small, pale breast tipped with a brown nipple. She smiled and spread her legs a little, her fingers digging under the waist band and rubbing herself.

I shut the curtain.

The worst part was…

Ah, shit. This is gross.

I… *ate* some of the dead flies in the window. The first couple made me gag a little, but after that it was kind of like tofu. Just spongy and flavourless.

I killed her, Julia. Oh my God, I killed her.

The prostitute, she was eating cheeseburgers, those little tiny burgers that come in a sack of twenty. She caught me watching her again, smiled, and tilted the bag toward me. I nodded. She stood and walked down the stairs to the car park.

I was trying to think of a way for her to get to the bathroom window, or wondering if she mashed those burgers down if she could slide them under the door, when she knocked.

"Hey! You the guy been watching me?"

"Yeah. Sorry."

She laughed. "It's okay. Can I come in?"

"I… I can't open the door."

"Is it stuck?"

"No. No, I'm—"

"You're afraid, huh? Like that Howard Hughes guy?"

She couldn't see me, of course, but I just nodded.

"Well," she said, "I'm Brie."

"Like the cheese?"

"Yeah, I guess. You hungry?"

"Uh-huh."

"That's what I thought. You looked hungry. I got this bag of burgers here I could share with you, but we got a problem. Can't get them in there without you opening the door."

"Yeah. I've been trying to figure that one out."

She laughed. It was a beautiful sound.

Then I heard the shuffling.

Then a thud.

"Brie?"

Then a wet slap, like raw meat being slammed on a counter.

"Brie!" My hand hovered over the knob, but I couldn't. *He* was there. *He* came for me. He took her just to get me to open the door. I know he did.

I stood there like that, useless, breathing heavy, crying, smelling those fucking burgers, and listening to this grinding noise, like rocks being forced into powder, on the other side of the door.

Finally he shuffled off down the hall, dragging her along with his useless leg. It sounded like her head was bouncing off of corners as he went.

When I was sure he was gone I cracked the door open just enough to yank the bag through, then slammed it shut and locked it. I slid a dresser up against it and sat on it, eating those delicious burgers from a blood soaked bag and knowing that I killed her. My stomach was—

BEEP!

Goddamn your fucking voicemail! Every fucking time! Fuck!

You're not coming, are you?

The walls finally spoke to me again. I asked about him, but they refused to say who or what he was, or why he was. Said it would anger him.

They did tell me what he did to Brie. It was so...

I threw up.

They warned me. Told me I had to leave. Said that he had a hard time getting into the rooms, but he would eventually find a way. They said I've been here too long, and he's noticed me because of it. They said he never sleeps. They said I have to leave.

They begged me not to tell him that they spoke of him.

What is this thing that even the walls fear?

He's outside my door. Julia, if you're coming, please hurry. I can hear him breathing against the door. I can see the shadow of his feet through the tiny slit under it. He's been there for hours. I don't know what to do.

I thought about calling the police, but what if they think I killed Brie? With my time in the hospital and your police report and everything...

Call me back so I don't feel so alone, okay?

He left, and I think that scares me even more. He slid a note under the door before he went. The writing's barely legible, like someone without thumbs who had to grip a pencil in their fist to write. It said:

They've been talking about me haven't they?

The walls asked me what it said. I told them. I shouldn't have. They've been hysterical since. One won't stop crying. Another has been praying the whole time. A third one curses me every so often, and the final wall just keeps telling the others to shut up.

Have I lost my mind again?

I managed to fall asleep earlier, but something startled me awake. It was a low moaning, like an animal in pain. I jumped out of bed and turned on the lights. I staggered back when I saw a line of roaches running down the wall.

When my eyes adjusted, I could see it wasn't roaches. I collapsed on the bed and prayed.

The walls… they were *bleeding*. That moaning, that was their death rattle. I sat on my bed, powerless, as the life slowly leaked out of them. The carpet soaked up their essence like a shag vampire until there was nothing left. The trails of blood left white streaks where it pulled the colour from that horrible flowered wallpaper. The streaks look like tears.

Now it's just me.

Julia. I love you so much. I don't know why you never came. I hope nothing happened to you. It's better to think you just stopped loving me, I guess. It's probably a good thing that you never came.

Sorry I'm whispering. I'm in the bathroom. He's in my room. I don't know how. I woke up when I heard the knob turning and rushed in here. He's trashing the room right now, throwing things, smashing furniture. He'll be in here before long. God in Heaven, I hope it's quick. Please, Lord, let it be quick.

Funny that I've finally found God, here at the end. You'll be happy about that.

I love you so much, baby. I'm so sorry I hurt you. I just wish that—

Fuck! He's at the door. Ohshitohfuckohshit! He's—

NO!

Hi! You've reached Julia's cell. Leave a message.

…

…

…

…JOOOOOL…YAHHHHHHH?

BRAD C. HODSON

BIOGRAPHY:

Originally hailing from Knoxville, TN, Brad C. Hodson currently resides in Los Angeles with his wife, actress Shannon Hodson. In addition to writing fiction, Hodson also heads up the sketch comedy group Happy Nowhere, as well as the fledgling horror production company Cat Scare Films. If you enjoyed *His Only Company, The Walls*, check out more of his work in the anthologies *The Age of Blood & Snow* (also by Morrígan Books) and *Midnight Lullabies*, as well as the magazines "Not One of Us" and "The Harrow." You can also look for him on Facebook (unless you are one of the faceless) and MySpace.

AFTERWORD:

Writing is such a strange process, and it's hard to tell where stories come from sometimes. Things often appear in my head — characters, plots, settings, dialogue, etc — and refuse to leave until I do something with them. These tiny little scraps of information usually become stories (sometimes they become nonsense, the literary equivalent of an abortion, but that's a different topic). *With His Only Company, the Walls;* the line "Walls can talk, you know..." was the entire impetus. That phrase came into my head, and I wanted to see what it was about. Then I decided to do something different with the first person narrative, and decided to play around with the idea of a series of voice mail messages.

I'm also a huge fan of the Stephen King short stories *1408* and *Everything That You Love Will Be Carried Away*. The thing that works with both of these are the sense of solitary confinement that you find within, that these poor bastards are trapped— not just in the rooms, but trapped by their utter "aloneness" (is that a word?). I wanted to try and capture that sense of isolation but do a very different story from either of those. What I ended up with was my own mentally askew protagonist, and a hotel that could or could not be haunted by something. I've had people tell me that they felt he was insane, others that the mysterious lurker was supernatural and only the walls a hallucination, others that it all actually happened. But I have to be honest: I don't know what's going on. It's not my job to know. My job is just to open that door labelled "Walls can talk, you know" and attempt to show what's on the other side.

REMAINDERS

1948

ROBERT HOOD

"Welcome to Hell."

As he stepped from the elevator onto the first floor landing, Mr Marcus Bryant Esq., explorer and hunter, thought he heard someone speak. He glanced around but the hallway was empty. That left the elevator operator.

"Did you say something?" he asked imperiously.

"No, sir."

Bryant stared into the dark-skinned man's eyes but could detect nothing except indifference. He dug a shilling from his pocket. The man — Indian perhaps, or an Islander — took the coin, nodded and slammed the metal concertina struts of the inner door. Bryant watched him through the grid until the outer door shut and the lift descended.

This hotel was making him feel uneasy. The elevator looked newly varnished but the lobby had been old-fashioned and somewhat tatty, originally decorated pre-World War One and never renovated since. It had an atmosphere of foreboding. Of course, it was clean — that was as expected, given the cost. However, Bryant hadn't felt comfortable with any of the staff he'd interacted with so far. To Bryant, their politeness hid a simmering, slightly *dirty* antagonism.

But beggars couldn't be choosers. He was here on business — financially desperate business. Hopefully the place would be upmarket enough to satisfy any investors he could entice into seeing him. The golden days of his rather exotic career — bringing down the largest of beasts with a single clean shot, being hailed as a Great Man in the salons of Paris, London, New York — were over now, rendered null and void by changing political and social mores. His desire to finance one last expedition into the Borneo jungles required him to tease money from investors and that in turn demanded an air of confident, even aggressive, success.

"*Show it to me*," a voice whispered.

Bryant glanced around, the suggestion of a figure lurking in his peripheral vision. But there was no one when he looked.

Without thinking he reached into his pocket and fingered the ancient metal object he'd bought from a cash-strapped street peddler a few weeks ago. It bore the symbology of a pre-Hindi Dayak spirit: an obscure animistic deity whose worshippers were rumoured to have horded the spoils of some ancient conflict somewhere in the mountains of Borneo. The artefact was said to be the key to unearthing their vast treasure. Bryant found its Asiatic curlicues — a jungle design that was oriented around two predatory eyes — both compelling and unnerving.

Something bumped his arm, causing the artefact to slip from his fingers and fall to the floor. Yet there was no one and nothing near him. He scowled at his clumsiness then bent down to retrieve the object. As his fingers neared its surface, however, he felt heat emanating from it and pulled away. But that made no sense. Could only be his imagination. Again he reached for it.

This time it shot away from his fingers, as though someone had kicked it. It rolled along the carpet, heading toward the shadows at the end of the corridor.

"Hey!" he yelled at nobody, as there was nobody else there with him. "That's mine."

Dropping his bag, he stepped aggressively after the artefact. It had disappeared from sight. He couldn't afford to lose it now.

An emotion very like panic, or perhaps despair, scratched into his gut as he neared the spot where it should have stopped. Worn carpet, that was all he could see. He glanced around, bending closer to the floor, straining his eyes as though he could will the carpet's dull floral patterns to yield up the thing he needed to find. Where the hell could it have gone?

Wait! There!

He could see it, a few yards away. Thank God! But as he went toward it, leaning to wrench it back into the safety of his pocket, it sank into the pattern on the floor, fading like late afternoon light. Bryant collapsed onto his knees, scratching at the carpet frantically with his fingertips. Nothing! The carpet was unbroken. There was no sign of the artefact. Nowhere it could be hidden.

It must have rolled further down the corridor.

He stood.

Something crunched under his shoe — a fern. Bryant kicked the squashed plant to show his contempt but the stem remained rooted to the spot. Frowning, he bent and pulled at it. To his surprise the plant appeared to be growing up through the dun-coloured patterns of the carpet.

What sort of place was this?

Light flickered. Bryant glanced ahead along the corridor as the glow from the evenly spaced globes stabilised. Some sort of alcove appeared at the corridor's end, perhaps housing a large pot-plant. At any rate, the lights had gone out completely and the shadows were multi-hued, suggesting that the furnishings were surrounded by decorative foliage. He hated artificial floral arrangements. Could his artefact have disappeared into that tangle?

He went to look and in doing so tore the plants aside. Nothing. Nothing at all.

As he sank back onto his haunches in despair, a whiff of dampness drifted into his nostrils; noticing it, he became conscious of an underlying rottenness — vegetative decay, the sort of thing you get in the sunless areas under a rainforest canopy. There was a hint of rotten flesh too, and sensing that, he felt his stomach heave. Fully intending to complain to the management as soon as he got to his room, and to demand that they find his property immediately, he glanced at the nearest door, noted the number and proceeded further along the corridor in search of his room. A house phone, that's what he needed. There'd be one there.

The stench got worse.

A reddish-brown object drew his eye. In a mass of ground vegetation that seemed to be sprouting from the skirting boards, was a large fleshy flower. He knew what it was: *genus rafflesia*. That would be where the odour of rotting flesh was coming from. The large parasitic plant, found throughout the jungles of South-east Asia, exuded a rank smell to attract insects such as carrion flies in order to help it propagate. It was nearly two feet across. How did they get it to survive here in a hotel corridor? And why?

What was that?

He thought he heard something, a distant cry that reminded him of monkeys. Sounded like a tribe of gibbons. He frowned. Ridiculous! Concentrating on the noise gave him a sudden awareness of the drone of cicadas, too — a susurration that rose from the lowest hearing threshold to a persistent buzz in an instant. Then weird grunts, roars, barks... What was going on? He could suddenly feel the lush heaviness of tropical humidity clinging to his face.

An insect bit him. He swiped at it, but was too distracted to aim properly. Ahead, the corridor had disappeared, transformed into a tangle of vines and tree trunks.

It was too much. Made no sense. Bryant backed away, turning when the walls that should have been at the edge of his vision remained a jungle tangle. But retreating the way he'd come did no good. There was no corridor at all behind him now, just a wall of vegetation. He felt panic rising in his gut.

A low snarl trailed out of the shadows.

Pulses racing, blood boiling in his ears, Bryant stood perfectly still. He knew what had made the noise — a leopard on the hunt. Big one, too, from the sound of it. It was impossible that a jungle cat should be here, in a hotel in the middle of a big Western city — but Bryant had no desire to attract its attention, impossible or not. He had no gun. His bags were lost. He listened as the cat padded, unseen, through the foliage on his left, circling. Oh, it knew he was here all right.

Anxiously Bryant took a step in the direction of the elevator. It had to be there, behind the impossible perplexity of the vines and jungle leaves. But tearing a path through the mesh of greenery merely led to more trees, more creepers, more liana.

Bryant could only function now by imagining that he had never been in the hotel, therefore hadn't been suddenly transported into the jungles of... What? Borneo? Was this Borneo?

You can't have what isn't yours.

It was the same voice he'd heard earlier. He spun around —
and bumped against someone. For a moment he thought he saw a
figure made of shadow and stray light — a man dressed in an old-
fashioned suit. The man stared at Bryant, a look of anxiety on his
face.

He seemed to be solid now.

"Do you work here, fellow?" Bryant asked. The man simply
stared. "What's wrong with this place?"

"Whatever is wrong lies in yourself." The man's voice sounded
distant. *"You brought the jungle with you. The hotel will use it against
you."*

"Use it? What do you...?" Bryant began, but at the end of a slow
though ordinary blink the figure was gone, leaving not a shred of
confidence in Bryant that it had ever been.

"None of this is real," he shouted. The sound was swallowed
up in an instant. He closed his eyes tightly. When he opened them
again the jungle was still visible, but diminishing, withering and
collapsing in on itself as though touched by some poisonous wind.

He thrashed out at the remnants, tearing at the blackening
vines and leaves, kicking at rotting flowers with his boots.

Then he was back in the hotel corridor, breathing heavily.

"Thank God," he muttered, staring along the faded carpet
toward the elevator.

Something moved behind him, signalled by a low growl
tangled in undergrowth rustle. He turned impulsively.

His mind registered dark, unforgiving eyes. A monstrous
humanoid body. Razor-sharp fangs.

The creature leapt.

Bryant watched his intestines spill out across the carpet for a
long moment before actually feeling the claws that tore them from
his flesh.

❧

It was the porter who found Mr Marcus Bryant Esq., the
famous explorer and hunter, lying dead in a pool of blood and
shredded flesh.

While waiting for the police to arrive and keeping curious

guests away, he observed the fear on the dead man's face and noted, too, the hand that had been torn off, its fingers clutching at nothing.

He smiled coldly.

BY THE HAND

PARIS

ROOM 206

TODD EDWARDS

When Celine Rockaway arrives at her hotel, she is already in bad shape. She staggers through the front entrance and has to lean on the bellman for a moment. He averts his face from the stench of stale bourbon and scented cigars as he helps her stand up straight. She lets him lead her across the lobby to the lift, and along the way, she stumbles as her high heels sink into the carpet. The staff fell silent as she entered, but she is too wasted to notice their attention.

In the lift, she jabs her finger at the button for the second floor, but she can't seem to hit the target. The bellman presses the button for her and then backs out of the lift. Celine has already slumped into the corner, propped up by the tarnished brass handrail. By the time she processes what has happened and thanks the kind bellman, the doors have already closed. Oh, well. She'll see him in the morning and give him a nice tip.

She focuses her thoughts and tries to remember which bellman just helped her, but the blinking lights counting up and up and up distract her. What was she thinking?

"Ding," she answers the lift and then giggles. When the doors open, she has a difficult time extracting herself from the corner. The doors close on her as she exits. The jolt focuses her for a moment. Room 206. That's where she needs to go.

The trip is short, but she doesn't make it. Halfway there, she stops to study an abstract painting. Oil on canvas. Vomit in planter.

Throwing up helps clear her head, but the after effects of the nausea make her shiver.

God, she thinks, *I need a hit.*

Back in the room, she splashes cold water on her face. It helps a little. It clears her mind enough to find her private stash of OxyContin. If Marcel knew she'd swiped them, he'd probably kill her, but hey, a girl's gotta live a little, right? She pops a few in her mouth and dry swallows like a pro.

Fifteen minutes later, she pops a few more as chasers. She wishes she had the good shit that releases over hours, but all she could get were the short doses. She thinks she is spacing them out, but she has lost all concept of time. She takes far too many.

She grabs the generic TV remote from the generic desk and plops into the generic armchair. Her head bounces off the cushion, and she smacks her forehead with the remote. She realises that it should hurt, but only a dull pressure makes it through the drugs.

After an hour of skipping around through late night cartoons and forensics shows, Celine feels ill. She struggles to stand so she can go to the bathroom, but the overdose of OxyContin interferes with the molecular workings of her muscles. She staggers against the bed as she walks.

The drug makes each breath a struggle — like sucking air through one of those little red coffee stirring straws. She giggles at the thought, but the strain makes her double over with a coughing fit. She reaches out to steady herself, but her legs give way, and she collapses in a heap.

Celine can't feel the floor. She's floating in a whirlpool watching the room go round and round. The sound of the TV fades as she sinks into the dark waters of the void. At the end, she wishes she could feel concerned.

❧

The sound of the door opening and a man swearing greet Celine as she rises back to consciousness.

"Goddammit, Celine. Get your ass up. What? Are you drunk? Have you been using my stock again?"

No, honey, just bourbon. The words form in her mind, but she can't make them come out. *What's happening? Why can't I talk? Why can't I move? Oh my God! Please! Marcel, what's happening?*

The pins and needles of sensation return in a wave that starts at her toes and flows up her legs to her torso. The excruciating pain makes her want to scream, but she can't move her lips. The sensation continues out along her arms into her fingers. She can't imagine a worse torture than to suffer the pain and not be able to move or cry out.

That is, she can't imagine a worse torture until sensation returns to her head.

The darkness grows into light as her vision returns, but she hasn't opened her eyes. They've been open the whole time. Now the dried out corneas burn like twin highway flares. She struggles to close her eyes, but the bland features of the room won't go away.

For months she has lived in the room with Marcel while he conducted his business. For months she has come home drunk or stoned every night. For months she has thought about dressing up the place, but who dresses up a hotel room? For months he has promised to finish up and return to Paris. He will take her and show her all the sights in Europe.

But for months, he's always had one more big score to make. And she's had to live in the same old hotel room.

And now she has to stare at it. She can't move or close her eyes. At least the pain from the returning sensation is subsiding. She cries to herself and wills tears to her eyes. It doesn't work.

Marcel's foot sets down in front of her face. Then his other foot comes, and he bends down to get a better view. It all happens in slow motion. He reaches out past her face and grabs her shoulder.

"Celine? Are you all right?

She can feel the strength in his hand as he squeezes, but Celine is detached from the process. She is just an observer, unable to respond.

"Are you going to get up and come to bed?" His voice sounds deeper and the words stretch out like they've been remixed by a DJ. He shakes her shoulder then stands up. "Fine. Have it your way. You can sleep on the floor like a dog. I'm wasted. I'm going to bed."

He does just that. She can see him undress and crawl under the generic bedspread on the generic bed. He turns off the TV and then the reading lamp. Celine is plunged back into darkness, but her eyes continue to burn.

Why can't I cry?

സ

When she awakes, Celine's muscles complain from having been in the same position all night. The urge to stretch is overpowering, but she still can't move.

What's happening? Am I dead?

But if she were dead, she wouldn't be able to feel the throbbing from where her hip and shoulder have been resting on the ground. Her dry eyes wouldn't burn.

She struggles to move or blink or form words, but no matter how hard she tries, the only result is a growing panic. She gives into the panic and mentally thrashes about while sobbing. Her body lies there like a statue the whole time.

It changes nothing. When she calms down, she is still in the same position. She can't even hear herself breathing. Her heartbeat is so soft and slow that she has to concentrate to detect it. She feels like a corpse.

Marcel wakes up and stumbles over her on his way to the bathroom. She can hear him peeing for what seems like hours. After he finishes, she can hear him mutter and curse as he approaches. Then he kicks her leg.

"Wake up, woman."

A long pause.

"Jesus, what did you take last night? Get up already!"

Another kick.

Rough hands roll her onto her back, and a wave of relief washes over her aching muscles. Marcel bends over and his face fills her vision. He stares into her eyes and then sticks his cheek over her mouth.

"Shit."

He slaps her hard enough to sting, but she can't respond.

"Oh shit, oh shit, oh shit!"

He grabs at her throat, and the panic rushes back as she thinks he's trying to choke her. Then it subsides as she realises that he is only searching for her pulse.

"No, no, no, no. Ah *mon dieu*! Stupid bitch! What have you done to me?"

From her new perspective, Celine can see Marcel sit on the edge of the bed, his face in his hands. Is he crying? Is he thinking? She can't tell.

Go get someone to help me, honey. Please!

Marcel stands and climbs into his clothes from the previous evening. He walks out of sight, but she hears his keys jingle. The door opens and then slams shut. At last.

Hope.

Staring at the ceiling for an hour gives Celine a new perspective on hotels. The office building sprinkler in the centre is the thing that taints the room and prevents it from ever feeling like a home. She hasn't noticed it before, but there it is, staring back at her. It hovers above notice, but subliminally it sends the message that you are in a corporate building, not a home. No home would have a sprinkler like that. And if any home did have one, there wouldn't be a placard next to it warning you not to hang anything from it. Homes don't have warning signs.

Focusing on the sprinkler helps Celine take her mind off of her troubles. The ache in her muscles subsides, and she grows used to the pain caused by her dry eyes. She just has to survive until Marcel returns with an ambulance or doctors or some shit.

God, I could use a drink.

The door slams open signalling Marcel's return. Celine can't tell how long he's been gone, but her spirits lift. Soon she'll go to the hospital and everything will be back to normal. Marcel is muttering, probably talking to the ambulance guys and being quiet so she won't get upset by what he's saying. Heavy things are being moved around. She can hear grunting and crashing as they move.

Then Marcel leans over her and checks her pulse again. He shakes his head and kisses her on the forehead. Then he reaches under her armpits and lifts her to his chest. Her view swings around wildly, and she can't tell who else is in the room. Why aren't they putting her on a stretcher?

Marcel carries her a few steps and then drops her. She falls in slow motion as she processes what she is seeing. Marcel stands over her looking sad. Not trying to catch her or break her fall. Down she goes. Dark blue walls rise up around her, and then she hits the bottom.

She stares up out of a pit as Marcel stares down. He looks like he's at a funeral staring down into an open grave while she's in the casket looking up.

Marcel! Please! What are you doing? Where are the doctors?

She doesn't understand what's going on.

Now he grabs her legs and shoves her into the foetal position.

By the time he has her stuffed into place, she is edging closer to panic. When he checks to make sure the lid will close, she loses it.

Oh my God! He's shutting me in some box! Marcel! Don't! Please, God, don't let him do this!

But he continues to work. Now she can hear him dragging something over to the box. What is he doing?

He grunts and then comes into view. He's holding a big plastic bag. Before she can see what it is, he dumps it on her.

White crystals like cloudy ice pour out. Smokey vapour envelopes the crystals and swirls around in the bottom of her container. Through the vapour she sees Marcel lift a second bag. Before more crystals fall, she can feel the cold of the first batch. Her dress doesn't offer much protection, and everywhere the ice touches her skin, needles of pain pierce her nerves.

More ice pours in. And more. And more.

She is covered in ice, but it doesn't feel wet. It doesn't offer any relief for her dry eyes. All it does is freeze her skin. The needles of pain turn to spots of fire. The ice burns like hot coals. The agony of being frozen alive shreds her remaining sanity, and Celine's world becomes pain and silent screaming.

Marcel puts the cover in place and everything goes dark. The pain continues, unabated.

Then, gradually, the pain recedes. Celine's thoughts slow down. She floats away from her body and drifts in a dark void.

She thinks of Paris. Relaxing at a café and drinking a glass of wine.
Ah, Paris.

TODD EDWARDS

BIOGRAPHY:

Todd parks his keyboard in many of the fine coffee shops in San Francisco. When he isn't writing, he travels around the U.S. and sometimes to Europe to repair robots. He grew up reading everything from Edgar Allen Poe to J.R.R. Tolkien to Richard Feynman, and his breadth of writing interests reflect that varied background. He writes both novels and short stories, and his genres include Horror, Fantasy, Science Fiction, Comedy and Thriller. He has also been known to mix two or more of the above. His short story, Paris, for the Voices anthology is his first published work outside of the realm of science journals. You can read some of his short stories and one of his novels at his website: www.toddcedwards.com

AFTERWORD:

I've spend many nights in hotels while travelling for work. One evening while visiting a customer near my wife's hometown, my mother-in-law asked where I was staying. I told her, and she said "Oh, isn't that the place where they found the body?" It turns out that police had found a body that had been stored in dry ice for a year in a room in the hotel across the street from where I stayed. When I heard about Voices, I knew what I had to write.

JUST US

ROOM 213

PETE KEMPSHALL

Room 213, 6.27am

Every crime scene is a story told backwards. One look is usually enough to tell you the ending: something's taken, someone's hurt. Someone dies.

Working out how the story started — that's the trick.

Alex Gallagher covered his nose against the stink — coppery, with undertones of a poorly maintained toilet block — and assessed this latest bloody climax. Even before he got at look at the body, he could tell the attack had been frenzied; several items of furniture had been shattered and the walls were a nightmarish Pollock, random crimson arcs spattering the cream, slightly dated decor. The corpse itself, oozing gently onto the drop-sheet, had been hacked so brutally it was almost in pieces. The chest alone had been stabbed so many times that it had taken on the spongy consistency of trifle.

But he'd seen worse. Ten years as Inspector Hoffman's DS, of course he'd seen worse.

Whenever anyone found out Gallagher was Hoffman's number two, the question was always the same: what's it like working for a legend? Because that's what Hoffman was — Sherlock Holmes made flesh. Gallagher had stood on the sidelines time and again as Hoffman had examined a murder site; watching as the man sucked up the horror, metabolising it. And every time, without fail, the unflappable Hoffman would get his man. The media loved him, his investigations always front page news; if Hoffman was on your case, you were going down, end of. Nothing stopped him, nothing deterred him. Nothing fazed him.

So to see him standing there like this…

Gallagher was used to being marginalised by the detective,

ignored until Hoffman wanted something fetched or carried, but this… Not once since Gallagher had walked into the room had Hoffman even looked up from the corpse. He just stood. And stared.

And shook.

"Sir?" Gallagher murmured. "Sir?" The spell broke. Hoffman turned red, wet eyes on his bagman. "Uniform are on their way."

Hoffman took a deep breath. "All right," the older man sighed. "Let's get on with it."

❦

Room 213, 5.15am

The porter stops struggling. The metal has cut so deeply into his wrists that blood is trickling from the abrasions: it's pooling in his palms, dripping to the floor whenever he flexes his fingers. But for all his effort the chair and cuffs hold firm. He's going nowhere. All the anger, all the frustration he's been holding in suddenly boils up his throat, distilled into a single, sustained note and howled out into the room. He roars for a good half a minute, before finally the cry falters and chokes off into silence.

The man watching him from the armchair is unmoved — the combined effect of the gag and the heavy sack that he's placed over the porter's head means that no one outside the suite will have heard. It's a pointless defiance, a waste of time and energy. So he simply waits, watches, until the porter slumps forward at last, exhausted. Defeated.

Then, and only then, does the man in the armchair silently stand. There's a gentle susurration of material as his legs rub against the upholstery, the only indication he's even there.

It's enough: the porter's head snaps up, seeking. The thick Hessian covering his eyes has effectively blinded him, but now he knows for certain he's not alone.

So much the better, thinks the watcher.

He considers what must be running through the porter's mind, the myriad possibilities for personal jeopardy being played out in his captive's imagination. And he smiles as slowly, deliberately, he walks towards the helpless youth, one soft footfall after another,

70

shoes sighing into the carpet.

When he steps on it, the plastic sheeting rustles crisply and the porter starts to struggle again, shouting into his gag. Casually the watcher backhands him, snapping the man's head to the side. Redness seeps into the sacking, up near the forehead. The watcher walks behind the chair and briskly, violently, yanks off the bag.

Free at last from the stale atmosphere inside the sack, the youth sucks in lungfuls of air through a nose bubbling with snot. Sweat and blood have plastered his sandy hair to his scalp and he blinks bloodshot eyes, trying to assimilate his whereabouts. He knows the room, of course — double bed, mini-bar, TV cabinet — he's probably seen it a thousand times in the course of his duties. Never like this, though.

He twists his head from side to side, and it amuses the watcher to think of the action as a silent plea: *no, no, please, don't do this*. Of course, the watcher realises that the porter is just trying to look over his shoulder, catch a glimpse of his abductor. Maybe he hopes to commit his captor's face to memory, just in case he can escape and identify him to the authorities. More likely he thinks that making eye contact will somehow affect his situation. He's no doubt steeped in those cheap thrillers where the victim sways the attacker by forcing him to see them as a human being, not an object… yes, maybe the lad thinks that'll work.

It won't.

The silent observer considers a moment, and walks round in front of the chair.

The porter's eyes widen as they take in his captor's surgical mask and cap, his disposable overalls and rubber gloves. Almost in spite of himself the watcher feels a flower of warmth bloom inside his chest — it's exactly the effect he'd wanted.

He wanders over to the table, picks something up. He's gratified when the porter starts to scream into his gag again. Gratified, but not surprised.

After all, it's a big knife. Very sharp.

The watcher plays with the blade, lets the light catch it for a moment as he tests the edge. But then it strikes him that he's slipping into cliché, and so he puts it aside, resting it lightly on the table again. Instead he pulls up a chair. The legs leave trails in the thick pile of the carpet, and he has to lift it off the floor when he gets to the plastic sheet, to avoid rumpling it. Delicately he perches on the edge of the seat. He leans in and aligns his masked face with the porter's, just centimetres away.

"Please," the watcher murmurs, voice muffled by the mask, "no more screaming. You know this hotel; you know how thick the walls are. No one can hear you and no one is coming to save you. It's just us now."

The porter makes no sound beyond panting raggedly. Good enough, the watcher thinks. He sits back, folds his arms. "You are Anthony Mitchell. You are a bellboy here. You work the night shift, nine til six." He lets the silence stretch.

At last, a nod.

The watcher reaches over to the table — Mitchell tenses again. But the watcher leaves the knife where it lays, instead picking up a white card rectangle. He sits, staring at it, lost in thought. After a moment, he holds it up directly in front of Mitchell's face.

It's a photograph, a luridly coloured image of a woman, hands cuffed behind her back, gag in her mouth. A sack lies in the gutter near her head, from which her eyes stare, frozen; it's a look that the watcher has seen oh-so-many times before.

And there's blood. A thick, tacky ocean of it.

"You recognise her," the watcher says. It's a statement, not a question — he already knows the answer. Mitchell shakes his head: no. There's confusion in his eyes. The watcher grabs him by the jaw, forces the snapshot closer to his face. "Look again."

Mitchell's shaking a little as he nods. The watcher's breath hisses through his nose. He seems to relax. "Thank you. I appreciate your honesty."

"She stayed here at the hotel. In this room, I believe. You carried her bags here, didn't you?" the watcher asks, although again, it's not really a question. He shifts his weight in his seat. Gets comfortable. "The police talked to you, you were their prime suspect for a while. Then the hotel's closed-circuit ruled you out, proved beyond any doubt that you were right here when the woman was being taken."

He tuts, changes tack. "Do you read the papers? No? You must watch the news…? You should. Keep you up to speed. If you did, you'd know the police are nowhere near catching the man who did this. He's just too clever for them, took care of every little trace that could be left behind. They didn't find a thing on the body, Mitchell. Not a hair, not a fibre, not a single speck of saliva."

The watcher stands, padding softly across the room to peer through a crack in the curtains. "A man as careful as that would have to be pretty confident he'd got away with it. With no physical evidence at the scene, there'd be nothing to finger him. Unless there was something he'd forgotten. Something he'd no knowledge of, so couldn't have taken into account.

"Something like a witness."

The watcher turns from the window, looks into his captive's eyes, sees the fear. "Yes, all it would take would be for someone to see him. If someone reliable could place him at the scene… well, it'd be all over, wouldn't it? All that planning, all that care. Wasted. You can imagine how that would feel, can't you?"

He strolls back to the table and delicately takes hold of the knife. Beneath the gag, Mitchell starts to snort. "So it would be very, very careless for a murderer to miss something like that. Leaving a witness alive, that's about the biggest mistake a killer can make."

The watcher pads around behind the chair. "You do remember her, don't you? Jennifer. Redhead. Tall. Died a week ago." He expects Mitchell to turn his head, try to follow him with his eyes, but the porter stares ahead, shaking. "A friend of mine was driving home that night, Mitchell. Passed within a few feet of where Jennifer was taken — about the same time she was taken, too. It stuck in his mind, you see, because someone walked out in front of him and if he hadn't been paying attention and braked just in time… well, the guy would be dead, the speed my friend was going.

"Thing is, this friend of mine — good friend, reliable — he got a very good look at this jaywalker. Looked him right in the eye, he says. Young man. Your height, your build.

"Your face."

Mitchell shakes his head so vigorously that tears and snot fly from his face. The watcher claps a hand to each side of Mitchell's head, arresting the motion and forcing him to face front. "I don't know how you did it, turning up there when those CCTV cameras put you here, how you faked that footage. But I've known my friend more than ten years, and I trust him. I trust him with my life. And if he says you weren't in the hotel when Jennifer died, I believe him like I saw it myself.

"Except that's not proof, is it Mitchell? One man's word, no matter who that man is, against solid evidence like the CCTV... If I left it up to the courts, you'd walk."

An ammoniac stench rises from the chair. Mitchell's finally wet himself.

"And you know I can't let you walk."

Mitchell's scream is cut off as the watcher falls on him, punching the knife into his chest again and again and again, thud after thud after thud. Blood sprays from Mitchell's nose. The watcher feels it stippling the skin around his eyes that's not covered by his mask and cap. Mitchell thrashes in his seat, and the chair topples backwards. The watcher lets himself tip with it, straddling the youth, each thrust of the blade now with his full body weight behind it. Thick strings of gore fly from the tip of the knife on the upswing, painting the walls. Mitchell gurgles, eyes rolling.

By the time the watcher stops stabbing, Anthony Mitchell is long dead. The watcher would have kept going, but the knife handle is slick with blood, and slips from his grasp the last time he tries to pull it free. He looks at it, sticking out of the Mitchell's chest. The torso is a ragged, pulpy mess and the sight jars the watcher. He stares, and tears well into his eyes as he moves his covered lips to Mitchell's ear and whispers gently.

"Jennifer Hoffman was my daughter."

∾

Room 213, 6.28am

Alex Gallagher reflected that the cuffs were probably unnecessary. Not only had Hoffman immediately called in and confessed, his spirit was obviously broken by what he'd done; he wasn't going to run. As the uniforms led the inspector, cowed and silent, from the hotel room, Gallagher couldn't help thinking how his former boss looked faintly ludicrous in the surgical gear he'd worn to scare Mitchell — to make the porter feel a fraction of the terror Jennifer had experienced. He hadn't thought Hoffman the type to resort to sadism.

Plainly, Hoffman was full of surprises.

Alone in the room now — Mitchell's corpse excepted — Gallagher paced to the window and peered out. The media vultures were already circling, news vans pulling up across the road from the hotel, disgorging camera crews. Hoffman would have to endure the ignominy of the 'blanket over the head', unless the woodentops could somehow get him out the back way unnoticed.

"You going to talk to them?"

Gallagher turned to see DC Brighton waving at the window with a pen. "They'll want to talk to you."

Of course they will, Gallagher thought. *Me arresting Hoffman... it's like Robin slapping the cuffs on Batman. They'll lap it up.* "They can wait," he said. "CIB'll want filling in first."

He'd already worked out his answers to the inevitable questions that the suits at Complaints Investigation would throw at him. Yes, he'd told Hoffman he'd seen Mitchell outside the hotel the night Jennifer was killed, despite the CCTV footage to the contrary. No, he couldn't prove it, but yes, he was 100 percent sure it was Mitchell. Yes, he should probably have informed the investigating officers first, instead of running straight to Hoffman with the information. And no, he'd had no idea that Hoffman would take the law into his own hands like that, even if he knew his daughter's killer would walk from lack of evidence. He'd never — *ever* — thought the inspector would go after Mitchell himself.

Hoffman had always been so... 'by the book'.

"Um... sir?"

Gallagher snapped back into the room. "Still here, Brighton?"

"I was just wondering... with the inspector, you know, out of action... that'd make you—"

"Christ, they've just carted him off," Gallagher snarled. "Show some fucking respect."

Brighton went the colour of the drop-sheet and bolted from the room. Already the uniforms were thinking of Gallagher as Hoffman's heir apparent. Everyone always thought Gallagher would be DS forever, that Hoffman would keep working until he dropped. Now suddenly, out of nowhere, it was Gallagher's time in the sun. He was going to be the one to whom everyone tugged their forelocks.

At last, after all those years in the background, *he* was Batman.

He waited to be sure Brighton was gone, eyes on the door. Then he sighed, looked down at Mitchell's corpse. "Alone at last, huh?"

Snapping on a latex glove, he gingerly opened the tattered remains of the porter's coat, slipped something — a locket hanging from a broken silver chain — into the inside pocket. A week ago, the necklace had hung around Jennifer Hoffman's neck.

DS Alex Gallagher — *DI* Alex Gallagher — smiled at Mitchell, put a rubber-clad finger to his lips. "No one else needs to know, right?" he murmured.

"Just us."

PETE KEMPSHALL

BIOGRAPHY:

Pete Kempshall lives in Western Australia and has written a number of stories for Big Finish's *Doctor Who* and *Bernice Summerfield* ranges. His only previous hotel story was about bumping into the Cigarette-Smoking Man from The X-Files in an LA lobby — but since the only other witness to that event has since vanished, no one ever believes him. You can check out his website at: www.tyrannyoftheblankpage.blogspot.com

AFTERWORD:

Just Us came from the notion that in a hotel anything could be happening in the next room down, and you'd be none the wiser. Someone could be facing imminent death, knowing that help is just the other side of the wall... but that it might as well be on the other side of the world. Originally written with a supernatural element, that part of the story was ditched in the edits in favour of a more down-to-earth menace (and is undoubtedly stronger for it). After all, who hasn't felt the metaphorical knife slipped between their ribs by someone looking for a pay raise...?

A PICTURE OF DEATH

ROOM 221

SHANE JIRAIYA CUMMINGS

The body dangled in complete stillness, a macabre centrepiece to the flurry of motion around it. Men in blue jackets, wearing latex gloves, prodded at the carpet with tweezers and arcane-looking devices. Their eyes were anchored to the ground lest their glance stray to the girl's face. She wore a mask of agony — bulging eyes and an endless scream locked in swollen white-blue skin.

"She died slowly, Detective — and painfully."

Detective Taylor was the only man brazen enough to stare the corpse in the face. "I can tell."

"Her neck didn't snap. She choked to death," the young Examiner added as an afterthought.

The scratches gouged into her throat and the blood beneath her nails had already told him that much. The girl's weight had pulled the noose so tight her throat was constricted to half its natural size. A purple bruise encircled her neck like an ink stain. Escape would have been impossible.

"What else can you tell me, Doc?"

"Not much, I'm afraid." The ME's eyes darted — she was a rookie, still unsettled by the sight of violent death. "I'll have to get more equipment from the van first. Can you have your men help cut her down?"

"Just need to take the photos, but yeah."

Nodding briefly, the ME hurried from the room.

Taylor's eyes traced the line of the impromptu noose, a pair of pantyhose, till his gaze hit the ceiling. A panel had been removed, allowing the pantyhose to be looped around a sturdy water pipe.

"Did the neighbours hear anything?" Detective Taylor asked of Ashton, his offsider.

"The couple in 223 didn't hear much, sir, just a muffled thud around midnight."

"And on the other side?"

"Not occupied, sir."

"Found some sand," one of the forensics called out.

"Hmmm. Bag it." Taylor turned back to Ashton. "The manager?"

"He's downstairs soothing some of the guests. He seemed pretty tight-lipped but said none of the staff had been near the room tonight."

"Brilliant," Taylor seethed. "Not a friggin' clue then."

"No, sir."

One of the forensic techs slid the balcony door open as he returned from outside, allowing a breeze, cold as death, to sweep into the room. The corpse rotated ever so slightly.

The girl swayed on the noose, inspecting the room with bulging, vacant eyes.

Detective Taylor glared at a tech edging away from the girl's feet. "Christ, can we get that photographer in here so we can finish this?"

"He's coming now, sir," said Ashton, as he peered out into the corridor.

Nodding to himself, Taylor tore his eyes from the body and busied himself with examining the room. It was neat — the bed unruffled, her suitcase still unpacked, nothing out of place. No signs of a struggle. Not a damn clue to be found.

From the corner of his eye, the fruit bowl painting above the headboard caught his attention. He walked over to it and ran a gloved finger along the gilded frame. The painting was free of dust, but like the girl, it was suspended lop-sided. Idly weighing the thought, his gaze wandered from the picture back to her.

She faced him — a dangling room ornament staring directly at him. Her eyes belied her scream, bearing a personal accusation.

Her momentum tilted her, with agonizing slowness, away again. She took her accusation with her.

Taylor swallowed a few breaths before returning to the painting. Momentarily transfixed, he appraised the gaudy colours captured by the artist. The more he studied the picture, the more his head swam. He blinked a few times to wave the feeling off. Before tearing his eyes away, he straightened the frame, easing one niggle in the process.

As he scanned the room, the incline seemed to tilt like a carnival fun house. He steadied himself against the headboard as he fought sudden nausea. The forensics moved around in crazy arcs, while the corpse floated before his eyes like a butterfly trapped in blurred slow motion.

A blink brought everything back to sharp, sudden focus.

"Sir, are you okay?" Ashton asked. "You look a bit pale."

"I'm fine," Taylor snapped. Wobbly at first, he returned to the centre of the room.

The photographer knelt by the bed fiddling with his camera.

"Everything alright?" Taylor asked, now steadier with something to focus on.

The photographer nodded as he continued to fumble.

"Mike," a voice called from the doorway.

"What is it, Dave?" Detective Taylor turned to face his partner, who was handling the legwork downstairs, free of the responsibility of supervising Ashton and the forensic technicians.

"Did Ashton fill you in on the manager?"

"Yeah."

"Good, cos I've just found something. Looks like our girl was into witchcraft. Seems she liked rituals and stuff, according to a conversation she had with the manager. Brought a bag full of mumbo jumbo up here tonight."

"Witchcraft?" Ashton sputtered. "The manager didn't say that earlier. Where's this bag he mentioned?"

Taylor berated Ashton with a glance, which silenced the younger man. He'd talk to him later about the oversight.

"Could be a link to occultists. Thanks, Dave. Anything else we need to know?"

"Yeah." Dave stepped closer to murmur. "Can you feel that tingle? Like electricity or somethin'."

Taylor nodded.

"It stops once you step out into the corridor."

Taylor nodded as if the statement made sense.

"It's true," a female voice whispered from behind.

"What?" Taylor spun around.

The girl swayed from her noose, still studying the room eyes that glistened in the light — the only female in the vicinity.

"Mike," Dave said, "What are you doin'?"

"Oh, ah, nothing."

"Mike?"

"It's nothin' Dave. Just thought I heard something, that's all."

"Alright. Take care up here then. I'll head downstairs and see if the staff know anything else."

"Thanks, Dave," Taylor called, as his partner disappeared into the corridor.

"Holy shit!"

Taylor spun around to see the photographer scrambling away from the body, with fear plastered on his face. Stuttering nonsense, he lodged himself into the corner, his hands flailing at the walls, his eyes darting.

"What the fuck...?" Taylor managed.

The photographer stammered and pointed towards the girl. The man's face was ashen; his eyes bulged like the corpse's. "Oh God!" he screamed, before huddling into a ball.

The forensics stood as one as a chill swept the room. For a moment the girl was forgotten as every eye was fixed on their gibbering colleague.

"What is it?" Taylor moved to stand over the photographer. "What did you see?"

The man stammered but refused to look up.

The girl's presence filled the room, stealing every vestige of warmth. Taylor could feel her, swaying, staring, as she dangled behind him. He ignored the sensation as best he could.

"Sir?" Ashton murmured.

Taylor's gaze was locked on the photographer. "We could all do with a break. Clear the room."

"Come on, guys," Ashton prompted, rounding up the forensic technicians. "Let's go downstairs."

Some of the forensics had already edged for the door, their kits in hand, well before Taylor's order. The relief on their faces was palpable.

"Detective, what about him?" Ashton pointed to the photographer.

"Get him outta here. See if the ME has something to calm him down."

"You there," Ashton called over a couple of the stragglers. "Help me with him."

"No," Taylor corrected Ashton. "You're staying here to assist me." He turned to the two techs. "Thanks. When he starts makin' sense, tell Detective Lewis to get a statement."

One of the techs nodded, before pitching an arm around the photographer's shoulders. The man's body was limp, offering no resistance as he was dragged away from the room. With their departure, only Taylor and Ashton remained. The girl's presence lingered throughout the room.

The stillness was brooding, a smothering blanket. The aura of men seemingly erased from the room. Taylor watched the girl tilt from side to side on a breeze long subsided.

Ashton moved a little closer to Taylor. "Sir?"

"We start at the beginning." Taylor studied the corpse as he spoke. "The girl checked in around 8.45 pm."

"Right, and from there came directly to the room."

"Yes, but not before having a chat with the manager about witchcraft."

"Yes, sir." Ashton agreed, still embarrassed at his oversight. Unlike the seasoned Detective, he didn't have the nerve to spare more than a glance at the body. He kept his gaze to the floor or on Taylor's broad back.

"So we have her in here for three to three and a half hours," Taylor prompted.

"Yes sir. Confirmed by the guests next door. They heard the thud when she was hung—"

"Hanged."

"Sorry — hanged — and they called the manager just after midnight."

"So, death occurred around midnight. No sign of an intruder. No one spotted anyone coming or going on this floor?"

"No, sir."

"That leaves us with the bag. Where the hell is it?"

"No sign of it so far, sir. Maybe the killer took it with him?"

"Probably..." Taylor stepped closer to the body, gauging its position in the room.

Ashton remained silent. He had worked with Detective Taylor long enough to know when he was concentrating.

"Something's been bugging me ever since we set foot in this room," Taylor said at last.

"Yes, sir?"

"We know she couldn't have killed herself. There's no chair under her, or other prop that she stood on. How high do you make the ceiling?"

"Umm, about four metres. This is a fairly old hotel, high ceilings and all."

"Exactly. How the hell did our perp get that noose around her neck and then pull her up so high? There's no shoe depressions on the bed, and that chair over there is just too damn short."

"I don't get it. Maybe the perp brought his own ladder?"

Taylor glanced back at him, not dignifying the proposition with an answer. "He'd also need amazing strength. Clearly the victim was still conscious and struggling."

His gaze lingered at her garrotted throat and the network of scratches and claw marks there. Trickles of dried blood encrusted her neck and disappeared beneath her dress.

"It's cold in here, sir. Can we turn up the heat?"

The comment drew his attention away from the girl's lacerated throat. "What do you mean? You're sweating like a pig."

Ashton dabbed at his forehead and then held his hand in front of his face, scrutinizing it with slack-jawed surprise.

"Go get some fresh air," Taylor chided, without the customary hard edge to his voice.

"Yes, sir." Ashton's teeth chattered.

As he turned for the door, his foot knocked something metallic on the floor. It clattered and tumbled across the carpet. Ashton bent down and retrieved it — the photographer's camera, discarded in his madness.

"I hope it's not broken," Ashton muttered, holding it up to inspect for damage.

Taylor watched his eyes widen, his face drain of colour.

Ashton trembled as he looked through the viewfinder, his pale eye magnified by the camera's glass viewing cube. His pupil dilated as he stood transfixed, watching something beyond Taylor.

Ashton whispered something, too quiet for Taylor to hear. Tears welled in his eyes and rolled unbidden down a face abruptly drained of colour.

Taylor rushed forward and smacked the camera from Ashton's grasp. It smashed into the wall, landing in a heap atop the night table.

"What were you lookin' at?" Taylor blocked Ashton's field of vision. "What was it? What did you see?"

"The girl," Ashton murmured, over and over again. Tears now streamed down his face.

"Come on," Taylor said, "Let's get you outta here."

Steering Ashton toward the door, Taylor's grip held him from turning back to see the visions unhinging him.

Half guiding, half dragging him through the door, Taylor spied the familiar face of Dave emerging from the lift further down the hall.

"Dave, a hand please."

"Shit, what's goin' on?"

"Not sure." Taylor handed the wilted form of Ashton to his partner. "He and the photographer saw something."

"Shit, Mike, first you clear the room, now this? This won't look good."

"Hang it, Dave."

Dave shot him a hard look.

"Sorry, bad choice of words. Look, get him downstairs. I'm gonna poke around for a few more minutes before we seal the scene."

Taylor met his partner's eye. Dave nodded. In moments he was ushering Ashton to the lift.

Turning his back on their retreat, Taylor clenched his fists, steeling himself for whatever lingered in room 221.

He stepped back inside the room and closed the door behind him with deliberate ease. The latch clicked into place. The air had grown icy, seeping in from hidden cracks to penetrate deep beneath his skin.

The girl had stopped moving. She hung in abject stillness, staring at him from beneath wisps of black hair. He'd never noticed her hair before, its shine, the way it caught the sickly fluorescent light from the lamp over the bed. Extraneous details often clouded the big picture. He was a big picture guy, caught up with understanding the pieces of the puzzle.

He took in every facet of the room anew, from the unruffled cream-colored duvet to the floral-accented beige curtains, and the colourful framed prints dotted along the walls, trying to let the pieces of this puzzle slot into place on their own. As he concentrated on the details, the vertigo returned. Subtly at first, but soon the carnival fun house was in full swing. The corner writing desk, the chair, the bedside table and lamp all spun through his vision like a lunatic whirly-gig. At the edge of his skewed perspective, the ochre walls heaved in sympathy.

At the centre of it all, the girl hung in stark immobility. The contrast was striking — the white, almost glowing, figure of the corpse suspended at the centre of a vortex of earthy colours. Nausea squirmed through his stomach and burned up his throat; Taylor squeezed his eyes tight against it. The dizziness followed him into the darkness.

Smells invaded the blackness. Rotting fish. Mouldy fruit. Burning plastic. The rancid amalgam of stench clashed with the burn at the back of his throat, forcing an involuntary gag. As he clenched a sweaty palm across his mouth, the world toppled.

He opened his eyes. The vertigo instantly abated. He lay across the bed, its softness enveloping. The wall prints, the ceiling, everything, were all back to their familiar rigidity.

He turned with hesitation to gauge the position of the corpse.

She stared down at him from her noose, leering through strands of raven hair.

He flinched. "Shit."

No matter where he was in the room, she was always facing

him, glaring at him, always. Goosebumps played along his arms, despite the sweat caught in his sleeves.

He weathered the scrutiny of her eyes as he struggled to rise from the fluffy duvet. It was soft. Too soft. Its folds held him, pulled him down.

Flailing to free himself from the duvet, he bumped the camera on the nightstand. The clatter of plastic and metal was a beacon of clarity, honing his attention to a fine wedge.

The duvet abandoned its fluid embrace as Taylor sat up and reached for the ruined camera. He muttered to himself as he moved to the outer extremity of the bed. Perched at the edge of the mattress, barely sitting, his legs bore most of his weight.

With the camera to focus on, reality constrained itself to something resembling normality. The nausea and vertigo had subsided, as had the smorgasbord of foul odours. He turned the camera over and over in the hope of deciphering its lunatic spell. Broken mechanisms rattled inside.

She bore holes of accusation and contempt into his turned back. His flesh prickled at the sensation. Her gaze was cold, like icicle raked down his back.

"Enough already!" Taylor glared over his shoulder. The glare was met with indifference.

As the broken camera rattled in his hands, another sound — like a buzzing of flies — prickled at the edge of hearing. He turned the camera, over and over, in response to the droning swarm as it intensified. The flies' buzz rose became incessant, rising to a fever pitch until at last he wrung his eyes closed. Cupping his free hand to his ear, he slammed the camera down onto the nightstand.

The thud silenced the swarm.

Sweat pooled under his arms and along the expanse of his back. His shirt was saturated. Heat radiated from him in waves.

In the ensuing silence, his gaze lingered on the camera. Something about it lying there on the nightstand, battered and broken, tugged at his thoughts. He pondered it for countless heartbeats; his eyes idly traced the lines of the electric lamp bolted to the wood, the notepad nearby, and the faded doily beneath it.

The nightstand draw was slightly ajar. That nagging feeling

persisted.

Instinct kept him focused solely on the nightstand. Concentration was his shield. He worked the draw open with meticulous care. Inside he discovered a dusty *Gideon's* Bible.

A corner of white paper jutted from the yellowing pages. The contrast was too obvious to be ignored.

The air, threatening to suffocate, abruptly stilled. As he reached for the Bible, a palpable weight lifted.

From somewhere behind, a soft intake of breath.

An icy draft caressed the nape of his neck like a lover's whisper. Not daring to be deceived, he cradled the Bible, allowing it to rest in his lap. In his own time, he eventually opened the book at the trespassing paper. The cold zephyr — spidery female fingers — moved to his ear. He hunched his shoulder in defence.

He snatched up the paper and absorbed himself in this clue to the girl's death. It kept his mind from the chill playing up and down his spine. The note read:

9:15 — I've just entered room 206 and I am noting my actions here should anything go awry. I've marked myself with the runes of protection before I even set foot in here, so I should be safe for now. The manager distracted me with talk of the haunted room next door and other strange goings on, but I'm determined not to let my concentration waver. I'll need every ounce of strength I can get if I'm to rid the world of this evil.

10:10 — The sigils have been laid. A protection circle in the centre of the room. More runes on the walls and carpet. I hope the manager won't mind too much. The room looks like a mural, but at least I'm doing the universe a favour. Blessed be!

10:40 — It's started! At first I thought I was just tired and my eyes were playing tricks. Then I realised it was the first manifestations. It attacked my circle straight away, trying to trick me into breaking the seal. I know it's testing me, so I must stay on guard.

11:20 — It's been half an hour but already feels like a lifetime. The assaults are constant now. The room pitches and sways. I see things. Weird things. My incantations are holding it at bay, but I have no idea if they're having any effect. Must fight on.

11:45 — It's getting desperate. So tired. Can't fall asleep.

11:58 — Mum, I love you.

Taylor skimmed the passages again and compared them with the note that followed. The entire room was freezing, chilling the patches of sweat infused into his shirt. The girl's sightless stare continued to gouge into his back. Reading her last thoughts only fuelled her scrutiny. He refused to turn and acknowledge her, choosing instead to engross himself in the note.

It went on:

To everyone one I love and cherish,

I have dabbled with witchcraft for too long. I know I have sinned against God with my blasphemies, and I need to be punished. I am a wicked little slut. A dirty, filthy whore. My sins have made me weak. I am pathetic and I don't deserve Jesus' mercy.

Goodbye world.

Taylor placed the note on the night table and pored over it with a critical eye. The last entry was crude, scratched in a hurried hand. The handwriting looked nothing like the first half. Not even close.

After scrutinizing the note for some time, his gaze strayed back to the Bible still open in his lap. His eye skimmed to the centre of the page.

It was the New Testament. Book of Matthew. 6.13.

And lead us not into temptation, but deliver us from evil: For thine is the kingdom, and the power, and the glory, for ever. Amen.

A loud knock at the door interrupted his reverie.

Taylor shook his head, closed the Bible, and stuffed it back in the drawer. He picked up the note, regarding it for a moment more before sliding it into his shirt pocket. He berated himself for not having a plastic evidence bag on hand. Sparing little more than a glimpse at the corpse, which had somehow lost some of its menace, he turned for the door.

"Mike?" Dave's muffled voice called from the other side.

"Coming."

As he moved for the door, he glanced again at the corpse. Her gaze no longer met his.

Within moments, the door was open, and Dave was staring him in the face.

"You look like shit." Dave offered a hand to help him outside.

As he guided Taylor through the door, Dave glanced over his partner's shoulder at the girl suspended by her own pantyhose. He averted his eyes, unwilling to meet her stare.

"Find anything?" Dave closed the door to quarantine the girl.

"This." Taylor produced the note.

"Suicide note?"

"Sort of," he stumbled down the corridor. In the open space, he felt reinvigorated. A world away from the claustrophobia of the room. "Let's get it down to the lab. This is gonna be a tough case. I can feel it going cold."

"A shame. I've only heard good things about this girl. The next of kin reckons she was a saint. We finished up here?"

"Yeah." Taylor adjusted his soaked shirt. He hesitated outside the closed door, intent on the gold numbering.

"You sure you're okay?"

"Yeah... This one got to me, Dave."

"Come on." Dave took his partner by the shoulder. "There's an all-nighter across the street. We'll grab a coffee while the ME and the uniforms clean things up."

Nodding, Taylor bade the door a final, fleeting look. The number 206 would be permanently locked in his mind. Even as he trudged to the lift, he could still feel the girl's stare at his back. Following him.

The lift door slid open and the two cops disappeared inside, locked behind sliding steel. The corridor fell deathly quiet in their wake.

✎

Through the fractured viewfinder of the camera, the girl's body was perfectly framed — the showpiece to a mural of runes and arcane symbols covering the walls. A scene missed by the police. A scene veiled to human eyes — a very different picture of death.

The room wavered like a heat mirage but was dark as if caught on the cusp of twilight. A sickly desert-orange light seeped in from the walls.

Darker shapes in the gloom, living shadows, yanked on the pantyhose noose and danced along the ceiling. The shadows swirled, time and again spearing their essence through the girl.

A broken circle of sand looped below her. An embroidered sack lay sprawled within the circle, its contents of new age bric-a-brac strewn across the floor.

Dangling above these, the raven-haired witch thrashed and clawed at the noose crushing her windpipe, her face contorted into a parody of a scream. She failed in agony each time the shadows pierced her soul.

She strained for another vision of the shadowy men half-glimpsed between moments of madness and searing pain. Men, and the world beyond, clear for the briefest of moments, highlighted by a tiny square window straddling her hell and the life before it.

The camera's viewfinder, the keyhole in the door, the loop of sash dangling next to the curtains, and the other cracks and holes in the room, were makeshift scrying ports — each a window, each framing a sliver of reality, bright and taunting in the gloom, forever and always beyond her reach.

SHANE JIRAIYA CUMMINGS

BIOGRAPHY:

Shane Jiraiya Cummings has had more than fifty short stories published in Australia, USA, and Europe. He is the author of *Shards* (forthcoming from Ticonderoga Publications), has edited several anthologies, is the managing editor of Black magazine and HorrorScope, has won two Ditmar Awards, and has been nominated for the Aurealis Award and Australian Shadows Award. Shane lives in Perth, Western Australia. www.jiraiya.com.au

AFTERWORD:

Stephen King has influenced almost every dark fiction writer for the last thirty years, and I'm no exception. When I first read his short story *1408* (long before it became a movie!), I was impressed with the way King could transform a mundane hotel room into something ancient and terrifying. The story lingered with me and a couple of years ago, the first draft of my homage to *1408* — this story — sprang from my mind fully-formed.

This story does not reach the terrifying heights of King's, but it did take on a life of its own in subsequent drafts, moving from homage into a more unique entity. The idea of combining a supernatural story with a police procedural had appealed to me, and this aspect became stronger when I rewrote the story. I hope you found it as unsettling as Detective Taylor and his team.

REMAINDERS

1968

ROBERT HOOD

Finding a hand was bad enough, but next to it lay what appeared to be a shattered eyeball. Sandra stumbled away from it blindly. Further back along the corridor the elevator door pinged. Perhaps it was the porter, bringing her luggage. She ran toward the central open area of Floor 2, the fact she'd dropped her handbag irrelevant in her panic. Her heavy-soled platform shoes thudded in the silence.

The elevator doors were open. As she stopped in front of them, gasping for breath, she saw that the car contained neither the porter nor the elevator operator. A man stood in the dim light, gaunt and silent. His dark, empty eyes stared at her.

"Sorry," Sandra said. "I thought..." She swallowed back the pointless explanation. "There's been an accident or something."

"*An accident,*" he repeated in a low, monotonic whisper.

"What?" She wasn't sure she'd heard what he said.

The man did not reply. Instead he looked her up and down, from her feet, up her bare legs to the mini-skirt she was wearing, to her knitted top, to the heart-shaped tattoo she'd had pressed into her skin at the base of her neck as an act of defiance directed at her parents, and finally to her eyes. His gaze might have been lascivious, but somehow she knew it wasn't. Rather, it was as though he were trying to commit her to memory.

"I think I was on my way to my room," she said. "I came across..." She leaned closer and whispered. "...Body parts."

She interpreted his unresponsive stare as scepticism.

"Come and see," she added, "Please."

When he moved he looked awkward and uncoordinated, as though his limbs hadn't had cause to function all that much lately. Even odder was when she turned from him to lead the way; in her peripheral vision it didn't seem as though his legs were propelling him along at all, rather that he was floating. She started in surprise and looked straight at him but the effect dissipated at once, as though it had never been.

"Sorry," she muttered.

This time she let him go first so she could keep her eye on him.

The hand was where she'd first seen it; seeing it again — coldly and directly this time — caused bile to rise in her throat. She choked as she swallowed it back. The hand hadn't been cut off but torn, the bone of its arm broken raggedly, the flesh still leaking blood. The blinded eye lay at the end of an opaque ichor smear, as though it had crawled, bleeding all the way, from the site of whatever violence had been inflicted on it.

The man picked up the hand. Displayed like that, held between his fingers, made it more obviously feminine compared to when it had been lying in its patch of gore.

"Shouldn't you leave it where it was?" Sandra asked, "For the police."

The man studied the eyeball for a moment then placed the hand on the floor — not where he'd found it originally but a few paces away, in a relative alignment with the eyeball — where it might have been had the body been complete.

He stood straight and stared at her.

"Which is your room?" he wheezed.

She pointed further along the corridor. "On this floor, I guess. I haven't been to it yet. I was on my way there when I came upon..." An involuntary glance at the hand made sickness rise again. "I thought the porter would be here by now. He was bringing my bags."

The man moved off down the corridor in the direction Sandra had indicated. It had been a random gesture, but he seemed to know which room was hers, even though she didn't. She had no intention of following, of course. She had to report this to someone in authority, someone less eccentric. That meant going down in the elevator and away from whatever the man would find further down the way.

"I'm going to get help," she shouted.

The man glanced back. *"You can't go,"* he said. *"Not yet."*

"What do you mean? Is there something wrong with the lift?"

He turned away and continued along the corridor.

Sandra left him to it and ran back toward the elevator shaft. The doors were still open — which in itself was a bad sign. If the elevator was working properly surely someone would have called it down by now. Anyway, didn't the doors close automatically if left alone for a while?

When she stepped into the car, she realised how old-fashioned it was. Perhaps the inner door had to be shut manually? But if so, who had done it when she came up? She didn't remember sharing the elevator with anyone.

Come to think of it, she couldn't remember coming up in the elevator at all. She must've been really out of it. All that hash she'd smoked last night...

She pulled the concertina door shut and hit the "Close doors" button. The outer doors remained open. She tried again. Nothing. She pressed the button for "Ground", but again nothing happened. She whacked at all the buttons this time.

Panic swelled in her stomach, agitating the bile again. "Calm," she whispered, "stay calm." Her therapist had told her that she had to stay calm in all circumstances. She was only 25, but had inordinately high blood pressure. It was the fault of modern society and its corrupting influence, her spiritual mentor, Starchild Moon said.

Wait! Stairs! There had to be stairs down to the lobby. She pulled open the inner door of the elevator, rushed out and looked around for an EXIT sign. There was one about ten yards in the other direction. Good! She rushed toward it, turned the handle — but the door wouldn't open. Filled with sudden rage, she began pounding, kicking, screaming.

"I've found more," the man whispered against her ear.

She shrieked and jerked away, back to the wall. Where had he come from?

"You scared me!"

"You must see."

She waved for him to back off. "I don't want to see anything. I want to get out of here."

"You can't — until you see."

His voice entered her head like a drug, dulling her resistance, overwhelming whatever logic might have driven her emotions up to now.

"But it's horrible," she pleaded.

"This place is a focus of horror," he said. *"You can't escape it when it makes demands of you."*

She followed as he moved off along the corridor, not wanting to go, but feeling a deep need to do so. She realised that she didn't know where this place was and had no idea why she was here. What had happened to her last night?

When they reached the spot where she'd found the hand, she noticed that the man had indeed collected more body parts: another hand, this one with the arm still attached; two feet, the left balanced precariously at the end of a leg, the other ripped off at the ankle; a hunk of thigh, the bone and flesh scorched where it had been torn from the rest of the body, as though by an explosion. There was also part of a shoulder and a head, turned to one side thankfully, so she didn't have to see what was left of the face. The man had arranged these scraps on the floor, laying them out in the approximate position where they would have been if the body had been whole.

"What are you doing?" Her voice was almost a cry of agony.

"They force me to show truth to those who deserve it." The sigh that was wrenched from his chest was so deep it resonated in her bones. *"I'd hoped that if I brought the pieces together I could stop it."*

"What do you mean?"

"As always, I fear I'm too late."

His trembling hand pointed towards the body parts, forcing her to look at them once again. Lain out in this poor imitation of a human form, the scraps of pale flesh and shattered bones — alternately torn, shattered, bloody and singed — were sad and pathetic. Tears welled in Sandra's eyes.

"It's awful," she whispered.

The man hunched down over the incomplete corpse, his hand pointing at the neck. Sandra tried to focus on what was there, though her vision had become blurred. What she could make out was a mark, obscured by the violence that had been committed on the flesh there. She involuntarily moved closer.

A tattoo?

"Please, you have no right to do this." The words came from between her lips like a moan wrenched from deep in her gut.

She saw the small, defiant heart.

It was just like hers.

The man glanced at her, his expression a shimmering mask of sorrow. Slowly he reached to the head, its auburn hair torn from the scalp in a patchwork of blood and burn-scars.

He turned the face towards her.

POSSESSIONS

CONSTANCE CRAVING

ROOM 301

GARY MCMAHON

"So, Constance, what exactly makes you think you're a vampire?"

The girl looked up from paring her nails, her eyes were narrow slits, and a dark, mocking smile decorated her face. Her skin was pale; ghastly, really, like a Halloween mask. Long dark hair. Kohl pasted around the strangely colourless eyes. Her ears were pierced, and in each lobe she wore a tiny black inverted cross.

"Well? I'm waiting, Constance."

"I like to be addressed as Connie." Her voice — no doubt along with her mind — was as sharp as a box of razorblades. I could not help but smile at her sophisticated use of language. She was thirteen going on thirty.

"Really?"

"Yes. And please stop smiling at me like that. If you don't stop smiling, I'll kill you."

I stopped smiling, but not out of fear. I will admit that her deadpan bravado sent a chill through my blood, and the way her own smile never wavered was unnerving, but I was not afraid of this frail-looking teenager. Not yet.

I walked around the room, examining the posters of pop stars and actors, taking note of the book titles on the shelves — popular novels by Laurell K. Hamilton, Anne Rice and Poppy Z. Brite. On the surface, this was the room of an average schoolgirl, but Constance had not been average for quite some time, and this was, in fact, a cheap double room in a nondescript hotel. She had been living here for a week, ever since the Intervention. Her terrified parents had been keeping her locked up like a criminal simply because they didn't know what else to do with her. They had brought in some of the girl's personal belongings and a few items of furniture, but the presence of none of these could erase the sense of impermanence, of temporary habitation.

The Reverend Alex Potter had asked me to come and talk to the girl. He was instrumental in her being here, having personally recruited Harvey Janus, the man the gutter tabloids had once called an "Exit Counsellor", to snatch her from the clutches of the cult she was involved with. Even now, thinking back, it was all pretty amazing: an ordinary schoolgirl caught up with a bunch of lunatic cultists who thought they were vampires.

I was just about old enough to have lived through the 1960s and been aware of the Charles Manson case. I knew how easy it was for vulnerable young men and women to get caught up in a web of drug-abuse, sexual terrorism and possibly even murder. Luckily, things had not gone that far with Constance, but that was only because they'd managed to get her out in time. It was apparent that several forms of mind control technique had been utilised and possibly a type of psychological or even physical abuse, but the details were sketchy at best. Constance was saying little; her thin, black-painted lips were sealed.

I walked towards the small table at which she was sitting, her attention once again devoted to filing those long nails. She'd tried her best to shape them into points, all of them, as if still trying to live up to the image that was only now beginning to falter. I admired her resolve, but the end result was rather shoddy, the fingernails broken and ragged, rather than sharp and sleek.

"I'd rather you didn't come any closer." She did not look up, just kept on with the low-rent manicure.

"And why's that, Constance?"

She stopped filing. Closed her eyes. My refusal to use her nickname was getting to her. Then she opened her eyes again and put down the small stainless steel nail file. "Because," she said, turning to me at last. "I'm still hungry. And when I'm hungry, I can't be trusted." She smiled, her lips drawing back across teeth sharpened to points. Not just the incisors, but all of them: the entire set. It must have taken hours and caused her a lot of pain. But, according to Harvey Janus, who knew about such things, each member of the cult was forced to endure similar extreme dental work in order to prove themselves worthy of being a member. That was the first step, the induction. What followed was much worse, and involved the blood of animals.

At first.

"Would you like a packet of crisps? Perhaps a nice ham sandwich from room service?" I tried to keep my voice light, sardonic, but there was no getting away from the fact that this entire situation was unnerving.

"You are such a silly little man. You all are: silly, silly little mortals. No wonder we treat you as cattle."

"Would you mind if I sat down? Not next to you, just opposite. In that other chair." I did not make a move in her direction, allowing her the illusion of control for the time being.

"Okay. But be warned, I'm fast. I can open up your throat in a heartbeat, and the next beat will send your blood rushing into my mouth."

I could tell by the smile that she liked that one. She'd remember it and use it again.

"Oh, *bravo*! Very Hammer House of Horror," I said, striding towards the chair and pulling it out from under the low wooden table.

"Since when did vampires like Take That?" I pointed at the poster of the boy band above her bed, trying not to laugh.

"It's all simply part of the game. If they think I'm cured, they'll let me out of this room and I can go back to my real family."

Her logic was flawed; surely a member of the Undead could open any lock, leave any prison cell? But I left it there, storing up the ammunition for later. Let her dig her own grave, I thought, with a smile.

Constance was a petite girl, not much taller than five foot, and her arms and legs were painfully thin. She was wearing a thin shift dress and black boots that came up to just below her knees. Her hair was naturally ash-blonde but, predictably, she'd dyed it black; her eyes were brown but she was wearing grey contacts that made her look even more like the commonly accepted image of the undead. As makeup effects go, it was a decent effort. She certainly looked the part, like an extra from a low budget horror film taking a break between scenes.

"Do you know who I am? I've been here for over ten minutes now and you've not even asked my name. Aren't you even curious?" I placed my hands on the table top to show her how steady they were. My fingernails were bitten badly and there was some light bruising still visible across the knuckles of the right hand. I'd just come off another job, one that had turned a bit nasty.

"Your name is Thomas Usher. You are forty-five years old and you are supposedly able to communicate with the dead." She resumed staring at her fingernails, inspecting her work. "Ghosts surround you all the time, clamouring for your attention."

"So the Reverend informed you of my background."

"No," she said, looking up and directly into my face. "He told me nothing about you."

My heart began to beat a little bit faster and sweat ran down the middle of my back. Constance impressed me more with each passing minute. Her performance was quite brilliant. I began to realise something no one else involved in the case had even bothered to consider: this girl actually *believed* that she was a vampire. She was not pretending; there was no artifice about what she was doing. Constance was absolutely one-hundred percent certain of her status as a bloodsucker.

This made everything so much more difficult. Despite my talent for seeing the dead, I possessed no way of knowing if she were telling the truth. As far as I was concerned, there were no such things as vampires, but I couldn't help believing in ghosts.

"Your parents are very worried about you. They think you're suffering from some kind of mental collapse."

Constance smiled, and held my gaze. "I, Mr. Usher, am a vampire. It's that simple. When we were on holiday in California I was abducted by a group of young devotees, disciples of a man whose name I can never repeat in public. They took me to him as an offering, as *food*, but he liked me. Apparently I reminded him of someone, a girl he'd once coveted. So he made me just like him."

Delusions of grandeur. She liked the idea of being unique.

"If that's the case, Constance, then you aren't really that special, are you? As far as I know there are at least a few dozen other kids just like *you*. Silly little moppets who've had their teeth ground down to points and who swan about covered in black make-up, biting cats and dogs."

Her eyes went hard and cold as steel. The skin around her mouth puckered, tightening, and she hissed. She *hissed* at me like a snake. "We do *not* drink the blood of house pets. It's part of the initiation. First, you take a cat or a dog, and then you move on to a person."

The room grew suddenly cold. The pipes leading to the radiator under the window began to tick, like a clock. I stood up and put my hand against the crenulated surface of the heater. It was freezing, not just cold: *freezing*. The room had been too hot when I walked in, but now it felt like a morgue.

"I suppose you did that? Made it so cold?"

"We like the cold." She kicked the leg of the table; her left hand slipped off the top and onto her knee, where she played with the hem of her skirt. She'd changed in an instant from angry, potentially violent young urchin to a sweetly sensual Lolita.

Her lips were bright red. I could have sworn that they'd been layered in black lipstick when I entered the room, but now they were the rich shade of fresh blood. I didn't see her reapply the make-up; I was certain that my gaze had not left her long enough for the change to occur.

"I don't mean to scare you. I just need a friend." She fluttered her eyelids and pouted those lips, slowly parting them. Her teeth were shockingly white. It was obscene.

"You're a bit young for me, sweetheart. I prefer a woman with hair on her arse."

Her hand stopped just as it touched the side of her head. Unbelievably, she'd been about to commence twirling her hair with her dainty little fingers. It made my skin crawl to think about where she'd learned to act like this, and the moral poverty of whoever had told her that all men respond to such blatant signals.

"What do you want from me?" The eyes were stone once more; the face a malleable mask.

I walked away from the window, resisting the urge to glance

outside. No matter how claustrophobic the atmosphere in the room, everything I was here for sat between its walls. For now, there was nothing out there for me. I had promised to stay here, as trapped as Constance, until I knew what made her tick.

"I just want to help you. Help your parents, and the Reverend." I sat back down at the table, examining for the first time since I'd entered the room the drawings she'd been working on. There was a box of crayons near her hand and the pages of a sketchbook lay torn clumsily from their binding. Upon the sheets she had coloured images of violence and bloodshed. One of the pictures showed a man with a white collar decapitated by a large dog. In another, two people, a man and a woman, were cut in half by huge hands wielding a scythe. The pictures were crude, childish, yet incredibly effective.

"You like my artwork?" She leaned back in her chair and folded one leg over the other. There were scabs on her knees.

"Don't give up the day job," I said, picking up a picture of a short-haired man cutting off his own arm with a sword. "You're not even on par with Tracy Emin, never mind Van Gogh."

She sniggered, but said nothing.

"Is this what you want to happen to them all? To the Reverend and your parents? To me? Is this what you'd like to see?"

"My mother and father, yes. The Reverend is already done for. As for you, I'm not so sure...you *amuse* me."

I gripped the edge of the table and pulled myself forward, trying to intimidate her. "What do you mean about the Reverend?" There was something about the delivery, the nonchalance of her tone, which made me latch on to exactly what she was saying.

"Why do you think he wasn't here to meet you? My folks are at home, holding hands and waiting to hear the outcome of our little chat, but the good old Rev was supposed to be waiting for you, in here with me. He was supposed to be the one to let you in — did you not wonder why the door was unlocked, leaving a teenage girl so vulnerable?"

She stood for the first time and I was surprised at how slight she actually was: I could see the bones of her thighs through the thin cotton dress and her hands looked too big for her skinny forearms. A light tracery of blue veins was visible through the papery skin, like a stylised henna tattoo; she looked as frail and insubstantial as an anorexic fashion model.

"I killed him for sport before you arrived and stashed the body under the bed. He was beginning to bore me." She ambled across to the bed and lay down on her belly, then rolled slowly onto her back, drawing up her knees but keeping them locked together, raising her arms above her head on the spongy mattress. It was yet another nauseatingly immature attempt at seduction, and if I didn't feel so uneasy I might have laughed.

"I don't believe that for a second. Even if you did go for him, the Reverend is a big man. He'd put you across his knee and spank you."

She sat up, so quick and agile, moving too smoothly, as if there were no bones in her back, and upon her face was a lascivious grin. "Maybe if he'd done that, he'd still be alive."

I let my head fall towards my chest, a great sigh pushing out between my lips. When I looked back at the bed she was gone. Just like that: like magic.

I walked over to the bed and stared down at the indentation in the sheets, and when I placed my hand there, the sheets were still warm. I looked around, but there was nowhere in the room to hide. It was too small, too compact and functional, and there were no dark corners to investigate. The bathroom door was open and I could see that she was not inside. The shower had no curtain to conceal her and there was nothing under the sink but a single drawer too small to contain much more than a tiny toiletry bag.

Constance was gone.

I'd only taken my eyes off her for a second; barely even time enough to blink. But when I'd returned my attention to her tiny form it had vanished into mid air.

"I'm still hungry," she'd said, teasing me. And maybe that's what she'd been doing all along, playing with me like a cat with a bug, leading me on until she tired of the game. But in that case, where was she now? How could she have gotten out of the room with me lodged resolutely between her and the door?

I looked at the door. It remained closed, still locked, just as I had left it.

The radiator made that same ticking sound as before, and when I glanced over I noticed the open widow above it. When I'd stood by the window earlier I was sure it had been closed.

I walked to the window and pulled it shut, wondering who else might be out there, in the shimmering twilight, perhaps waiting patiently for Constance to make her move before making their own. It had still been light when I'd begun my visit with Constance, but now it was growing dark.

I didn't notice the paper until I was about to turn away from the window. It was another of those sheets from the sketch pad. Something had been scrawled on it thickly, and in crayon, and then the paper laid face-down on the plastic sill to hide the words. I picked up the sheet and turned it over.

My lips went dry as I read what she'd written there in bright red crayon. The irony of the colour she'd chosen was not entirely lost on me.

you still amuse me
so you are still alive
let's keep it that way...
C

I folded the sheet of paper into four and slid it into my inside pocket, not really sure why I didn't just throw it away. I crossed the room and stood at the bottom of the bed, unable to kneel down and look under it for fear of what I might find. A man in a white collar, face pale, puncture holes in the side of his neck. Or another child-like drawing, depicting that very scene or one just like it. Perhaps that was even where Constance was hiding, the bedsprings digging into her narrow spine; face pressed to the floor, pale cheek in the dust. A mixed-up little girl pretending to be a monster... I was suddenly too afraid to find out.

So I turned away and walked out of the room, not looking back, never looking back, as I descended the stairs and walked through the lobby and into the street. Taking out my mobile phone, I decided to contact first Constance's parents and inform them that she wasn't in the hotel room when I arrived, and then the police to report two missing persons, a teenage girl and a man of the cloth.

GARY MCMAHON

BIOGRAPHY:

Gary McMahon is the author of two novellas, *Rough Cut* and *All Your Gods Are Dead*, along with the collection *Dirty Prayers*. His debut novel *Rain Dogs* is due out in 2008 as a limited hardback, along with the collections *Different Skins* and *How to Make Monsters*. Recently, McMahon has had stories selected to appear in *The Mammoth Book of Best New Horror* and *The Year's Best Fantasy & Horror*. His website is www.garymcmahon.com

AFTERWORD:

Constance Craving features my recurring character Thomas Usher, a down-at-heel working class man who happens to be able to see ghosts. In the stories, Usher comes across all manner of ghosts and earthbound spirits, but I realised that he'd never encountered a vampire. Perhaps he still hasn't. I wanted the story to be ambiguous about the existence of these creatures, and the typical teenage girl at the centre of things needed to embrace the pseudo-gothic trappings the media present as being associated with bloodsuckers. The chance to focus the action between these two characters in a single room appealed to me greatly; as someone once said, the essence of drama can be distilled to a couple of people in a room. When all is said and done, the question remains: is she or isn't she? I'll let you be the judge of that.

BEDBUGS

ROOM 321

MARTIN LIVINGS

The first bite happened just before midnight. At first the sting didn't rouse Allison from her slumber, her state of exhaustion so complete that she most likely would have slept through an army of vampires chewing on her limbs. But it persisted, and slowly she awoke, confused at first, disoriented. She groaned and slapped at her hand, at the annoying sensation there.

Something squished beneath her fingers.

She opened her eyes to complete darkness. At first she thought she was in her own bed, the bed she'd shared with Dan for the last seven years. She started to reach out to him, before her brain kicked in and reminded her that no, she wasn't in her own bed; in fact her own bed was no longer hers, hers and Dan's. Now it was someone else's. Someone else's and Dan's. The thought sickened her — her husband curled up against the back of another woman, the vague stirrings of a sleeping erection pressed against her buttocks. And all the while, she was here, alone in a queen sized bed in a cheap hotel room, at least until she could find somewhere to rent. It wasn't fair, especially as it was all his fault. But she hadn't wanted to cause a scene, and particularly hadn't wanted to spend another night in the house, their house; the house where he'd betrayed her behind her back, again and again.

She reached to the bedside lamp and fumbled for the on switch. It was one of those awkward types that required a dextrous twist right near the bulb, something she was barely capable of even when fully awake. It was a miracle she got the light to come on without sending the entire lamp crashing to the floor. She sat up on the over-starched white sheets, hotel sheets, hospital sheets; looked at her hand.

There was a bug squashed there, its body so ruined that Allison couldn't even tell what kind of insect it once was. Now it was a dead bug, a bloody bug. Her blood. The bite was already starting to itch. *God, I hope it's not a spider*, she thought as she reached for a tissue to clean the mess off her hand.

Another stinging pain erupted on her ankle.

"Shit!" she cried, and threw back the covers. This time the insect had already beat a hasty retreat, leaving no sign of its passing but for a nasty red welt right on the soft flesh just beneath the protruding ankle bone. "Shit!" she swore again. She pulled her ankle up onto her other thigh and examined the bite. It had a deep, glistening red dimple in the centre of it, and the flesh around it was swollen and itchy, just like her hand. She scratched it for a second, and then made herself stop. *That'll just make it worse,* she thought. *That'll just make it...*

—never for a moment, never again, my heart, my —

Allison gasped, her head jerking. The sensation was like waking up from a nightmare, head filled with unfamiliar thoughts. Her heart beat faster; her breathing was shallow and quick. She looked at the bites, the one on her hand, and the one on her ankle. Poisoned? Was this the first symptom? It didn't seem likely to her, but she was no doctor. Who was to know?

She looked over at the other side of the bed, at the telephone that sat there, wondering if she should call a doctor. It was bizarre, even now, with everything that had happened; she still slept on the left side of the bed, her side of the bed, even though nobody was sleeping on the right side anymore. At least not in this bed, this hotel bed. No, he was probably still sleeping on the right side of his bed, their bed, not their bed; no more. And on the left side... who? She didn't know, didn't want to know. Part of her wished she was still unaware of Dan's infidelities. If ignorance is bliss, then complete ignorance must be nirvana. But it seemed fate had conspired against her, against them. And now she was here, in a crappy little hotel room, alone, miserable, and possibly poisoned.

For a moment, she was so lost in these thoughts that she didn't feel the third bite, this time high on her thigh. When she did, she tried to remain calm. She carefully pulled up the t-shirt she was wearing as a nightie, one of Dan's that she'd taken when she'd left, and looked at her upper leg. It was a nice upper leg, well toned, not yet succumbing to the ravages of age and orange peel dimpling. Allison knew she was an attractive woman. She didn't understand why Dan had felt the need to stray.

On her soft but firm pale flesh, a small black bug sat, its needle-like proboscis embedded in her skin. She could almost see the blood being sucked up into its tiny body, like soft drink through a straw. Then it withdrew the spike and looked up at her, its multi-faceted eyes black as well, black and shiny like polished obsidian. It cocked its head to one side in a peculiarly human motion.

She slapped with her unbitten hand, and it burst like a miniscule, blood-filled grape.

"Fuck you!" she yelled at the dead bug beneath her palm. "Fuck you and the horse you rode in on, you little bastard!"

There was a pounding on the wall behind her head. Three bangs, then silence. She sat, shocked, then realised it was from the room next door. The occupant had probably been woken by her tirade. Allison held back a giggle, afraid that it would sound hysterical. She raised her hand from her thigh. The bug was just a mess on her palm, a rorschach ink blot of blood and legs.

I see Dan, my husband, the man who swore to love and honour me, I see Dan the man fucking another woman on my bed, she thought, eyes closing. *I see...*

...please, God, don't let him do this to me, not again, the belt and...

"Christ!" Allison spat, as her eyes snapped open again. Again, there was a bang on the wall, just a single one this time. She ignored it. Her head was spinning, like she'd had one glass of wine too many. She tried to focus, and grabbed another tissue from the box on the bedside table and wiped the blood off her thigh. The bite looked the same as the ones on her hand and ankle, a fiery red dot surrounded by swollen flesh. It wept a pale pink viscous liquid. "Jesus!"

She felt another sting, this time on her face, just beneath her eye.

"Fuck me!" she yelled, and slapped herself in the face. It made a horrible sound, one that made her shudder with both fear and memory. *That's crazy*, she thought, *Dan never hit at me, not once, never lashed out with his belt, over and over, first with the leather end, that wasn't so bad, but then he'd reverse it, and the metal buckle would whistle in the air, an early warning of the pain that was to follow, oh Garry, why...*

The thought was her own, and yet it wasn't, familiar as her own skin, alien as a stranger. She cried out and hauled herself off the bed. More bites came, at her face, her hands, across her back. One pierced her right breast, then another. A quick succession peppered her buttocks. She stood by the bed for a moment, arms crossed across herself, weeping from the pain. Then she reached out and grabbed at the blankets with one hand. She pulled it free.

The bed was swarming with them. Tiny black dots moved in intricate patterns across the starched white sheets, created complex Mandelbrots that collapsed in on themselves, then reformed elsewhere, never the same twice. Allison watched them for long heartbeats, horrified but fascinated. There seemed to be an overall pattern emerging from their continual shifting, a shape on the bed, outlined, crosshatched, silhouetted. It took her a moment to recognize it.

It looked like a sleeping person.

She turned and ran to the bathroom. Tears blurred her vision, tears and the flesh around her eyes swelling like water balloons being filled, ready to burst on some poor unsuspecting soul. She flicked the light switch and looked in the mirror. New tears joined the old.

Her face, framed by loose strands of her long, red hair, was a mess, covered in tiny crimson sores, each swollen and raw. At first it looked random, a horrible insect attack, but then she saw patterns there as well, straight lines, raised scarlet highway maps across her flesh, barely an inch wide. She reached down and removed her nightie, pulling it over her head, her breath catching behind clenched teeth from the pain. She stood before the mirror in nothing but her panties. There too, the red stripes of swollen skin, dotted with bites, across her breasts, her belly, her thighs.

"Jesus fucking Christ!"

She considered getting in the shower, but suspected that would hurt even more, hot water across all these tiny wounds, death by a thousand cuts. Instead, she took the glass that was next to the sink and filled it with water, needing a drink. She shook her head. *Look at you,* she thought to her reflection, *Jesus, look at you. Poor miserable Alice.*

No, wait. Allison. What…?

The phone in the next room began to ring, the one next to the bed. The glass fell from her hand and broke on the tiles at her feet into three large pieces. She turned to the noise, relieved to have been distracted from the terrible mess that was her mirror image. Someone had probably complained about the noise. She walked back out of the bathroom, towards the side of the bed. *I'll give them a fucking complaint,* she thought angrily. *Hell with the noise, I've been put in a room infested with bugs. I'll sue this fucking hotel for every cent it has, and more besides!* She skirted the bed, trying not to look at it. As she reached for the phone, she glanced at the sheets.

The figure on the bed was looking straight at her with the cut-out white eyes of a Halloween ghost.

She screamed, and her knees gave way. She tumbled forward onto the bed, still screaming. The wall behind the bed pounded again, and this time a voice joined in. "Shut up, you bitch!" the man in the next room yelled. "Shut the hell up! I'm tryin' to sleep in here!"

Allison didn't hear him as she collapsed face first into the bugs.

Silence and darkness swallowed her. She could barely breathe, and it was as if she'd been caught in razor wire, sharp edges jabbing every inch of her with equal parts viciousness and intimacy. She tried to scream again, but nothing came out, just a breathy gasp. She struggled, twisted and turned, tried to ignore the pain, the cuts, the jabbing. She looked around, for light, for anything.

A soft glimmer to her left caught her eye. She turned as best she could towards it. It was dim and speckled, light coming through a complex crosshatch of metal and foam. She reached out, felt wires slicing her skin lengthwise along her arms as she did so. Reached out, and grasped, and clawed. It was a ragged hole, framed by cloth, a pattern of red flowers circling its edges like a maypole dance. She grabbed the edges with bloody fingers and hauled herself towards the light.

Allison fell from inside the mattress to the hotel room floor, like a birthed calf left behind by its mindless mother. She lay there for a moment or two, curled up, the pain slowly receding. Once it had dulled enough, she shakily got to her feet and walked back towards the bathroom. She watched her feet as she walked. There was something wrong with them, something different. They didn't look the same shape as they once did. And the flesh seemed grey, flaking with each step.

She reached the bathroom and looked up at the mirror.

Her face was a rotted mess, the skin all but gone, peeled away by decay and bugs. The nose had long since been eaten away, leaving a gaping hole in the middle of her ashen, lifeless face. No lips remained, just the hideous smile of a skeleton. A few straggled threads of pale blonde hair hung down like creepers, as lifeless as the face they brushed. And the eyes... the eyes were a teeming mass of black bugs, their chitinous exoskeletons lending them a shine, a life they didn't actually possess. They tumbled down her ruined cheeks like black tears.

She screamed, finally, the sound filling her head to bursting. She staggered backwards out of the bathroom and collapsed onto the bed again. There she lay, completely still.

And she remembered.

Alice, yes, her name was Alice, not Allison. And Garry had brought her here, just one more time like so many others, brought her here and made love to her on this bed, this very bed. No, not this bed, not anymore. He had made love to her, but something had gone wrong, something always went wrong, and he got angry again. The belt slid from his pants, wrapped twice, thrice around his fist, then snapped out like a rattlesnake. Again and again it happened, like so many other times, but this time was different.

This time, Alice said no.

This time, Alice said no.

This time...

Garry always carried a knife, tucked into his boot. A wicked thing, he used it to scare away anyone who pissed him off. He'd never pulled in on Alice, though, never, not once.

Only once.

Still alive, still bleeding. The knife slicing the mattress now, sheets crumpled on the floor. Breathing shallower, shallower, then hands under her armpits, hauled towards the bed.

No…

Darkness. Cold. Death. But not quite death. Inside, in the dark, jagged womb, the bugs arrived, arrived and feasted on her, in her. Eating at her. Absorbing her.

It was three weeks before someone noticed the smell.

The cops had taken what was left of her body, hauled it from inside the mattress in several sizable pieces. The mattress was removed as well, used for evidence, burned. The room was fumigated. And yet some bugs survived, in the carpets, in the cracks, bred with one another. Carried her memory forward, always forward.

Another volley of thumps, this time on her door, brought her around. She sat up on the bed, still naked except for her panties. That voice again, muffled, angry.

"Will you shut the fuck up?"

She climbed off the bed and walked to the bathroom. She glanced at her reflection in the mirror. No bites, no bugs, her skin smooth, pale. Her face was Allison's, familiar and strange, but her hair was blonde now, not red, and her eyes, Alice's eyes, were calm. She knelt and picked up the largest shard of glass from the floor, still wet, and hefted it in her hand. It would do.

Alice strode to the door, Allison watching as her — their — arm reached for the lock. They felt neither shame nor embarrassment, just unspeakable excitement. The shattered glass was held tightly behind their bare back, jagged edge upwards against their spine. The man wasn't Garry, wasn't Dan, they'd have to wait.

Not long, lovers, traitors, they thought as one, and smiled a small, strange smile. *Not long.*

But for now, for starters, this man would do just fine.

MARTIN LIVINGS

BIOGRAPHY:

Perth-based writer Martin Livings has had over forty short stories in a variety of magazines and anthologies. His short works have been listed in the Recommended Reading list in *Year's Best Fantasy and Horror*, and have also appeared in *The Year's Best Australian SF & Fantasy, Volume Two* and *Australian Dark Fantasy & Horror: 2006 edition*.

His first novel, *Carnies*, was published by Lothian Books in June, 2006, and was nominated for both the Aurealis and Ditmar awards.

His website: http://www.martinlivings.com

AFTERWORD:

Bedbugs evolved in a very strange way. It was born, of course, from the idea of bugs in a hotel room, something that's always made my skin crawl. Somehow, that lead itself to the old urban legend of the body hidden in the hotel room bed. But the structure and content of the story when I started working on it was radically different to how it ended up in the final edit. I was stuck with it, unable to make it work, so I threw out everything I'd done and started from scratch, writing it in a single frenzied session, trying to capture the feel of a hotel room fever-dream instead of a more formal standard story structure. I was aiming for a David Lynch kind of feel, where reality and fantasy are interchangeable, and nothing is exactly what it seems. How much of the story actually happens is anyone's guess. All I know for sure is; hell hath no fury...

FAKING IT

ROOM 331

SIOBHAN BYFORD

The client was nervous and even more of a freak than usual; a bewildered mess of sweat stains and desperation.

Celeste didn't like it. She didn't like the stale air or the nylon curtains heaped in a dusty pile in the corner, or the stack of lampshades teetering like faded hats in a thrift store on the floor of the kitchenette. Great. The client was afraid of the dark.

She glared at Paul, her partner in crime, what was he thinking agreeing to a session in a hotel room? How could she deliver a convincing performance with sunshine and naked electricity lighting her stage, illuminating the tricks of her trade? Oh, well, she'd just have to insist on darkness. And a *lot* less noise.

"Do you think you could turn off the TV? And the radio?" Celeste shouted above the racket of a soap opera and a badly tuned mix of stadium rock and static.

The client stared at Celeste blankly, arms crossed over her chest, features cast into stark relief by the bare light bulb hanging over her head. She started to reach for the TV's remote control, but snatched away her fingers as if the table lamp's shadow burned.

Impatiently, Celeste pointed the remote control at the TV bracketed high above the bed like a bloated spider and slapped the clock radio into silence.

"If I turn up everything loud enough, it almost drowns out this hideous noise," the client covered her ears. *"Shut it. Shut it. Shut it."*

What noise? Celeste glanced sideways at Paul. He shrugged. She rolled her eyes. The dozy cow was hearing things. It wouldn't be the first time one of Celeste's fiscally retarded attention-seeking clients descended into hysteria. Well-adjusted people didn't tend to call on her services.

"May I ask, who did you lose?" Paul lent forward, meaty face marinated in sympathy. Bloody do-gooder actually believed this crap could help people. It was starting to be a problem. Hope, even false hope, had a price and if Paul wasn't willing to charge it then Celeste would find someone more suited to the clairvoyant trade.

"Myself." The client laughed savagely, slopping coffee down her crumpled T-shirt.

"Is there a history of hauntings in your family?" Paul calmly took the mug from her shaking hands. He switched on the plastic two-toned kettle. In Celeste's opinion, the client didn't need another coffee. The silly bitch was trembling.

"No. No, my problems began with work." She picked absently at one of the scabs dotting her bare arms.

Must have been working since she was twelve, Celeste thought cynically.

"I first noticed the... *presence*... at the hospital." The client spoke hesitantly. Lifeless hair fell over her face, brittle as asbestos. A stripe of premature grey marked the point when she'd stopped maintaining her black dye job — probably around the same time she stopped washing her clothes.

"I know how... strange... that sounds." She continued with aggravating slowness, "I first felt It in the room of an old lady who was admitted to hospital with severe exhaustion." She paused, staring into the corners of the hotel room, eyes darting, as if she were tracking movement in the shadows. She shuddered. "Her family asked me to see her. At the time no one knew why she was so drained."

Probably from listening to your muttering.

"Oh, you're a nurse?" Paul inquired, setting down three instant coffees.

"No, what I do isn't nursing. You could call it counselling, in a way, helping people overcome their fears."

Hard to imagine anyone paying to speak to this boring bitch. Celeste could barely stand it and she was getting a fee. She briefly eyed the cheque on the table, made out to cash and above her asking price. *Nice.*

"The distraction is too much. I haven't been able to work since that first day. I'm struggling to concentrate just to talk to you. I've tried to escape It; avoided all the places where I felt It seize me — It was bad at home so I came here…but that made little difference. I can't get away from this… *presence*, wherever I go I hear Its voice in my head. I'm sorry to drag you into this." She attempted a smile, dry lips cracking over yellowed gums.

Celeste put down her coffee. There seemed to be something genuinely wrong with this client, aside from being a nut job. She pushed her mug away, hoping it wasn't contagious.

"Have you seen a doctor?" Paul drained his coffee, germs and all. Paul had the constitution of an ox.

And the arse to match.

"Yes, she couldn't find anything wrong with me, not physically anyway…"

Now there was a doctor with low standards.

"So I went for a psych evaluation. And that made It worse, too many people giving It attention. I never put much stock in the wisdom of the old saying, ignore it and it will go away — until now. Not that It has gone away, but It's less maddening when I try not to think of It. And of course, one must never speak to It directly."

"Or name it, I imagine." Paul laid his hand over the client's, but she was staring at Celeste, expecting a response, the lines of her face stiff with apprehension.

"I understand," Celeste cooed. "There are unwholesome beings in the universe that thrive on attention," *they'll even pay for it, the losers,* "but Paul and I know how to deal with such creatures."

"That's what I hoped you say." Tears of relief traced mascara down the client's jaundiced cheeks. She hunched into a contorted shape, arms wrapped around her knees, casting a strange shadow on the blank hotel room wall. She looked up slyly, "I get so tired, I can't go on dealing with It on my own."

Celeste battled a strong desire to sneer. *Why the hell did these weepy women apply make-up like a three-year-old with a crayon? Did they think dirty tearstains lent them an air of tragedy? It was tragic all right.*

Paul patted the client's hand. "We'll need to turn off all the lights, and hang the curtains before we begin the séance."

"No!" She snatched her arm away. "It thrives in darkness. It builds Itself with shadow and sorrow. You'll need It weak to call It out."

Oh, for fuck's sake. Celeste smiled tightly, "Ok, we'll leave the lights on. Not a problem."

She'd just have to be extra careful with her little tricks.

"Form a circle and let the healing begin." Paul smiled encouragement. *Naïve prat.* The exercise was nothing more than an expensive placebo for a woman scared by the bogeyman. It was all in her head.

Paul and the client closed their eyes like good little children.

They all joined hands around the table; the client's grip surprisingly hard, a wiry strength vibrating through her slender limbs.

"I call upon the being haunting this woman to withdraw from her, never to return," Celeste began. The client was eating it up, jaw clenched, eyes squeezed shut. With shameless melodrama, Celeste intoned, "I, Celeste, servant of light and life, demand you appear to me, oh creature of shadows and sorrow."

Celeste was surprised to feel the surface of the table turn and slide under her arms. *Nice one, Paul.* That was unlike him, he usually took séances too damn seriously, preferring to let the 'spirits" put on a show unaided.

"Make yourself known to me, oh spirit." Celeste called.

The metal table leg collided with her knee. She stifled a gasp of pain and kicked Paul under the table. *Careful, you fool.* He frowned, but his eyes remained shut.

The client squeezed her hand tight.

Ok, ok, keep your knickers on, moron, you'll get your money's worth.

"I call you out, shadow creature!" Celeste raised her voice, "reveal yourself to me."

"Yes." The client sighed, "Oh, yes."

"I... Call... You..." Celeste growled as if the effort cost her dearly, "... Out."

Celeste's chair shifted under her, almost throwing her to the floor. She glared at Paul's impassive face. *You'll screw it up by going too far, idiot.*

"It comes!" The client opened her mouth wide, her tongue lolled to the side, she exhaled, a wheezing death rattle. Celeste gagged into her own shoulder at the foulness of the woman's breath.

A sickly sweet scent pervaded the room.

"It's happening; It's gathering Its form." The client whispered, eyes dancing.

"Of course it is." Celeste agreed, patronisingly, wishing she could rub her throbbing knee.

The client glared at her through a web of dry, dead hair. The menace in the woman's eyes prickled the fine hair on the back of Celeste's neck.

What the hell was she doing here, in this stranger's nightmare? The hotel room suddenly seemed unreal; a stage set that didn't quite meet at the edges. She refused to look at the walls — struck with an irrational fear they would come apart at the seams, exposing a crawling darkness underneath.

"Oh unnatural creature," Paul cried dramatically, "the great and powerful medium Celeste demands you be gone from this woman! You must answer her call."

Celeste turned her head sharply. She thought she saw something move in the corner of her eye. Yes, there, a dark blur scampering like a spider across the kitchenette bench top. And more, spreading across the bed and swarming the silent, flashing television — bugs, the dump was infested — but Celeste could not make out the form of the insects as they hovered, slivers of darkness, in the air.

The client dug her fingernails into the back of Celeste's hand, rapture on her sickly face.

Celeste barely noticed the pain, the skin across her neck, her scalp, and her chest felt too small, stretched tight and crawling with ants. Maybe the bloody client *had* made her ill.

The woman giggled.

Celeste caught her breath. Before her eyes shadows broke away in pieces from the corners of the room, curled and burnt, swirling up on unnatural currents to slap against the ceiling, leaving ashen kisses on the white plaster.

No. Not possible. It was some kind of trick, an elaborate hoax, the revenge of her former clients…

Celeste's denials trailed away as the shadows flowed together, coalescing into a vaguely human shape the colour of burnt meat.

"What's happening?" Celeste demanded; her eyes wild, voice shrill with anger. She tore her hands lose, breaking the circle.

Paul threw his arms in the air and swung his head from side to side, eyes shut tight, "We lend our energies to the brave Celeste so she alone may battle the Nameless One."

Stupid, fat, ignorant Paul, eyes closed to the problem, as usual completely oblivious to the situation.

It must be some kind of set-up, a trap to bust fake mediums….

"This one revealed you, this one called you out!" The client jabbed her finger at Celeste, a zealot at a witch trial.

Mad bitch, I knew there was something wrong with you.

"You have no power over me now!" The woman clapped her hands, a loud slap that echoed across the bare walls. The mass shattered and dropped onto Celeste's shoulders, momentarily blanketing her completely in darkness before It disappeared from sight, leaving the room unnaturally bright, drained of shadows.

Celeste fell forward, bent beneath the weight of the thing that clung to her back, just beneath her skin, crushing her with Its malevolent rage. The panic she felt in her mind did not reach her limbs; her body was too tired to respond to her fear.

No, no, no, this isn't happening. Slumped over the table, Celeste stared listlessly at the over-stuffed pillows and the sage green carpet, a veneer of comfort and normality, wishing the hotel's decor was more exotic, more gothic — if this…*thing*… could touch her here, amidst a backdrop of commercial blandness, nowhere was safe. It isn't real. *It isn't real. It isn't real.* Belief in the supernatural was for the weak and the delusional, not for her. She gave a laboured sob. The stench of her own breath sickened her.

"It is done." The client pushed the cheque across the table, under Celeste's nose. "Thank you, you've more than earned your fee."

Celeste stared at the cheque's fine print, at the name of the paying account, *Athena's Psychic Services*, but she was too distracted to register its meaning.

"Did the light go out for a moment there?" Paul asked; ignoring Celeste draped over the table. She knew he'd seen her strike more dramatic poses to conclude séances.

Celeste listened with the forced focus of a drunk trying to pass for sober, the tension in her body and the pressure in her head building to an almost audible force, droning like flies trapped against glass, filling her mind with static.

"Yes, but I've got it back now." The client picked up her suitcase. She clasped Paul's hand, "I can't find the words to thank you."

"Celeste?" Her name cut through the white noise. The client, silhouetted in the doorway, stopped to tell her something, babbling nonsense about heeding some old saying.

Celeste glared at the treacherous bitch, hating her. She could see her lips moving, slick with gloss, but she could not make sense of her words. Baby pink lipstick leaked into the tiny lines radiating from the woman's mouth, watery blood trickling out a crooked tracery from the edges of a wound.

Do babies have pink blood? The hissing in Celeste's head surged into menacing, utterly alien laughter.

The client softly closed the door.

SIOBHAN BYFORD

BIOGRAPHY:

Siobhan is an Australian writer whose speculative fiction has appeared in *The Outcast, Dark Animus, Shadowbox, Togatus* and *Antipodean SF*. Her non-fiction publications include museum catalogues, magazines and journals. Her writing has been performed on stage and short-listed in competitions - in 2005 she won the Australian Horror Writers Association's Best Short Story. Her drawings have been included in exhibitions and Siobhan is currently working on an illustrated fiction project and exploring North America with her husband.

AFTERWORD:

After seeing a late-night TV advertisement offering the services of 'genuine psychics', I began to think about a cynical character and the adventures she could have in the commercial world of genuine psychics. The hotel setting of *Voices* inspired the rest of *Faking It*. Hotels 'fake it' by selling the concept of a 'home away from home,' and hotels are often the setting for behaviour separated from the home for nefarious reasons like crime, adultery or dishonesty - and, conversely, for experiences elevated out of ordinary life such as honeymoons or vacations. But what of an experience of the supernatural — do we pretend it never happened, an illicit affair, or think of it as holiday magic, an escape from the everyday? Either way, if we leave it behind in the hotel it will never touch our real homes… or so we can hope.

REMAINDERS

1988

ROBERT HOOD

"People leave things behind all the time," the porter said.

"What sort of things?"

"Clothes, wallets, souvenirs... you name it. Possessions they forgot they owned."

Marc Gowing frowned ostentatiously. "Forgot they owned? What's that supposed to mean?"

The porter, aged somewhere between 28 and 58 going by his appearance, crinkled his lips in a way that bespoke contempt. His haggard weariness may have been the consequence of age or recent debauchery — it was hard to tell in the jaundiced light of the elevator. If Gowing hadn't already despised the man, he would have taken an instant disliking to him there and then.

The doors of the lift pinged open, revealing the depressing mid-market tackiness of the hotel's third floor. Gowing stepped out at once and the porter followed with his bags.

"What room was it?" Gowing asked with chilly superiority, refusing to look at him.

"328, sir." He gestured with a twitch of his shoulder, his hands being occupied with Gowing's luggage. "That way."

Gowing hadn't seen the gesture and rather than demeaning himself by asking for a re-enactment, paused to read a sign. It was halfway up the wall in front, below eye-level, and so dimly lit he had to lean over to make out the numbers.

"Go right," the porter sneered.

Gowing straightened, brushed at his coat sleeve and began down the right-hand corridor. Almost at once he could detect the same stale funk of low-grade floor cleaners you found in every second-rate hotel everywhere.

"Here for work?" the porter asked behind him, and added with a suggestive lilt to the last word, "Or pleasure?"

"It's none of your business," Gowing snapped.

"Just making friendly conversation, that's all." The porter's tone of wounded injustice infuriated Gowing so much it was all he could do not to king-hit the man with a blow to his obnoxious, pouting mouth.

The truth was, Gowing had no business being here and sincerely wished he wasn't. All he was doing was avoiding; avoiding his bankrupt electrical repair franchise, avoiding his debts, avoiding his wife's accusing looks, avoiding the implicit criticism contained in his son's every misdemeanour. Was it his fault that Daniel was a junkie and a social parasite? Was it his fault the pregnancy that resulted in Daniel hadn't been a welcomed one in the first place? Where does responsibility end? Gowing and Gillian had fought about some careless remark he'd made in response to her endless fussing over their worthless son; Gowing had tossed a few clothes in a bag and left. That was all. He didn't care any more, not for either of them — if the truth be told, not even for himself.

"Your room's just there," the porter said suddenly. "I've got work to do."

"Work?" Gowing turned to glare at him.

"I'm busy."

The porter, looking oddly perturbed, had dumped Gowing's suitcase at its owner's feet and was striding back down the corridor toward the lift.

"Hey, you're supposed to --"

"*Don't worry*," whispered a voice in his ear. "*Let him go.*"

Gowing steadied himself against the floral wallpaper — ten years' old if it was a day.

"Who–?"

He stared into the strangely dark eyes of a man standing less than an arm's length from him. The man was wearing an old suit — old in style, not in age. It was in mint condition. Where would you buy a 1920s-style suit like that, new? He was medium height and solidly built, though there was something frail and unhealthy about him. *Stretched*, Gowing decided. He looked as though he could remain where he was only through a continual effort of will.

"Do you work here?" Gowing asked. "Are you the manager?"

"*I was left behind,*" the man said. "*Now I walk these corridors... to help, if I can.*"

Gowing frowned at the ridiculous and decidedly awkward answer. What did it mean? "I'll carry my own bag," he said, grabbing the handle. The man's voice had been strange, like an echo in his skull. "I'll be okay from this point, thanks. I don't need help."

The man stared at him with unnerving frankness. "*Everybody leaves something behind,*" he said. "*What will you leave behind, Mr Gowing?*"

He had to be some sort of employee. How else would he know Gowing's name?

"Look, Mr... whatever your name is..." Gowing growled. "I don't have to have this idiotic conversation. I'm not in the mood for amateur philosophy."

The man bowed his head in acknowledgement.

"To be perfectly honest,' Gowling found he wasn't able to stop himself from continuing, "I have nothing to lose, nothing to leave behind. Everything I had is long gone."

The man sighed. "*Unfortunately there is always something to lose.*" He moved backward into a shadow, or became one. Gowing blinked and the man disappeared altogether.

"What the fuck?"

The lights along the corridor flickered and hissed, spitting like angry snakes.

Then the uneasy shadows thickened, revealing objects all along the walls, the floor, the ceiling. The images were dim and unclear but Gowing thought he saw travel bags, pairs of glasses, a camera, toys, watches, an iPod, dozens of books, shirts, dresses, underwear... and something else — a doll, no, it was squirming against the ceiling, floating... a baby, screaming...

A chill paralysis grasped onto his legs.

"What is th–?" he choked back his words as a woman's hand, the wrist clearly torn from the arm on which it had belonged, slid down the wall, hitting the floor with a dull *plop*.

Now there were sounds other than that of the baby. Gowing fell back, too numb to react beyond leaning against the wall for support. Sounds of fear. Passion that died even as it reached its climax. Anger. The choking wheeze of a young man's heart collapsing. The dark ecstasy of Ice as it mingled with blood...

He heard a whisper of Daniel begging for help as he sank into troubled unconsciousness.

Tears came then.

"I'm sorry," he wept.

Darkness swirled around him and took the breath from between his suddenly bloodless lips.

EPIPHANIES

SENTINEL

ROOMS 402-403

SONIA MARCON

Room 402

Morning. The two in the bed start moving. They arrived yesterday evening. They had been all over each other like they had just met, but were talking like they knew what the other wanted. No words of love shared, only instructions of lust.

Him wearing a wedding ring, her not.

It's not unusual for a lady to forget her jewellery. She hadn't forgotten the rest of her trinkets. Obviously, they are not married to each other. He is married to selfishness, she is married to ignorance.

They are both in this room out of fear, not passion. Fear of the knowledge that something they want is forbidden and inexcusable, so it must be closed off from the world. People make things so difficult for themselves. Now they're getting dressed into yesterday's clothes. This excursion was obviously planned to be externally ignored.

Would a wife think twice about a husband coming home on a Saturday morning still dressed in his work suit? It seems he doesn't think so. That's what he told Miss Peroxide last night. "My wife has the baby to worry about," he had said. "She's used to me staying out with workmates on a Friday night."

People who are a living cliché should be shot.

Pam should not have to clean up this atrocity; disposing of the evidence because she has to. Lovely Pam.

They dress in near silence. She asks when she can see him again. He replies with a shrug. She asks if he is happy at home.

"You don't ask me that. It's none of your business." He speaks without eye contact while putting on his shoes.

"I worry about you. I want to make sure you're ok." She is

rifling through the pile of jewellery she put on the bedside table the night before, systematically replacing each piece on her body in the reverse order she removed it.

He stands and walks to the full-length mirror on the wall next to the bed, attempting to smooth down his hair. "You don't need to worry about me." He walks around the bed to the other bedside table where he collects his wallet and keys, before returning to where she sits on the bed. He leans down and kisses her. "I'm going away next weekend. It's Nicole's birthday. I'll give you a call when I get back, probably next week." He kisses her again then straightens and smiles. "It's my turn to pay for the room." He leaves, closing the door behind him.

She stays sitting on the bed looking down at her hands. She takes a ring off her left index finger and slides in on two fingers down. She stands in front of the mirror to see if wearing a wedding ring would suit her. "Why can't I say no to him? Why can't he say no to me?" She wipes away the tears that have started in her eyes and swaps the ring back.

"I fucking hate him." She picks up her bag and leaves. She doesn't close the door behind her. There is nothing else that needs to be hidden.

Room 403

Another family; this one with accents. Eastern European? They dress like everyone else. Every-tourist-one else. The little girl is gorgeous. Taking everything she sees in like it's her first day with vision. She circles the room, inspecting the wallpaper with a small smile on her face. Her lips are moving like she's whispering to someone only she knows about. Her eyes' expressions give the same impression.

Children don't need doors to hide behind.

The gaze of the outside world does not crush them. It will eventually ruin her and turn her inwards: like her parents. It's the closed doors that steal innocence — the idea of privacy that creates fear.

The son is older and another fearful cliché. His clothing says that he is angry at everything. Possibly the fact that he must grow to be scared. The parents talk to their children in their home language. It's nice to listen only to the tone of voice, rather than the words. Tone can say more than words ever can.

The parents put their luggage on the double bed. The daughter finishes her round of the room then puts her small purple suitcase on a single bed near the opposite wall, while the son throws his on the ground near the other single. The mother talks sternly to him and he picks up his bag and places it on the bed. It is obvious the outside world has already ruined the parents.

The door to the room is open so anyone can see their children's behaviour and most parents would prefer strangers to witness perfection.

Room 402

Here is Pam. She walks into the room and sighs. She knows exactly what has happened. She pushes a trolley covered with linen that she leaves at the open door. She enters the room, strips the bed, bundles the sheets together and pushes them down the laundry chute. She leaves the room and returns with a vacuum.

Pam deserves all the beauty in life. The stars from the night. Christmas beetles in a flowerpot. But instead, she has to wipe clean the secrets of the disgraced.

Pam is not ruined by the outside.

She sings to herself as she pushes the vacuum around the room. The door is still open. She doesn't care who passes and hears. She's the kind of person who would make herself breakfast in the nude, whether she's home alone or not. That is beautiful. Fearless.

She finishes vacuuming, wipes down the surface tops of the bedside tables and then turns to the mirror. She looks at the reflection of the bed. Pam chuckles and shakes her head, before wiping the mirror down. She goes into the bathroom and sees that it's unused apart from the rubbish bin, which she empties. She walks to the door and turns, looking around the room, smiling.

She winks and then leaves, closing the door behind her.

Room 403

"Hello, miss. Could you help us, please, to choose a map?" The mother's English is good but broken. Pam stops by their door. The father is sitting on the bed surrounded by maps, while the son is looking out the window and has something like music blasting from a small personal stereo. The daughter is sitting on her bed reading a story to a small, green animal doll. She is not secretive about talking to an inanimate object, speaking loudly and changing voices for each character.

"Of course," Pam smiles warmly, "and my name is Pam, not miss."

The mother looks embarrassed but returns the smile. "Oh, I am sorry. I am Svetyana. This my husband, Ivor. This our first time in your country." She turned to her daughter. "Lydia, wees rustig." The daughter looks up at her mother like she had been slapped in the face. She continues to read quietly to her toy, which makes it obvious what her mother had said. Svetyana turns back to Pam, who is smiling.

"Well, I'm happy to welcome you," says Pam. "What can I help you with?"

Svetyana turns to the bed. "We have too many maps. We were worried that we get the wrong one, so we get them all. Now we are just confused."

Ivor says something in their language. Svetyana answers him then turns to Pam. "I am sorry but my husband speak English worse than me. So I talk so he will not be embarrass." She turns to her husband who pokes his tongue out at her. Pam laughs.

"He understood that ok." Pam has a wonderful jokey tone.

Svetyana laughs. "Yes, he understand well, but does not speak well."

Pam nods. "I can tell you, though, that your English is fine. May I come in?"

"Oh, please!" Svetyana moves and Pam enters. They both walk to the bed and begin quietly discussing maps.

Lydia has finished her story and is now sitting cross-legged on the bed, talking directly to her stuffed animal. Her face says that she is explaining something very important, and she moves her head in response to what her toy asks her. Suddenly, she looks straight up at the wall. She stares for what feels like forever. There is no fear in her eyes, but her head tilts slightly askew, as if she is the one now listening. She turns to her mother and speaks. Her mother ignores her and continues to discuss maps, so Lydia tries again. Svetyana turns and speaks angrily to Lydia, and then turns back to the bed.

"I'm sorry. My daughter is not so rude normally. She is curious about new places."

"That's ok." Pam looks over at Lydia, who is back staring at the wall, the doll on her lap also staring. "Is everything all right?"

"Oh, she is just playing. She says her doll wants to know if there are ghosts in this hotel." Svetyana smiles and shakes her head. "She has such imagination. But she should not interrupt."

Pam looks directly at Svetyana. "Some people have said that they've heard things. But I think everyone feels that way in a new place." She looks down at the maps. "I hope I've helped you."

"Oh yes!" Svetyana says eagerly. "Now we know we need only one map. Thank you so much."

"My pleasure," Pam turns to leave and Svetyana follows.

"May I ask about what you say earlier?"

Pam turns. "Yes?"

"About that people have heard things. In this room?"

"Oh, no, not in the room," Pam smiles, "I think most guests just aren't used to having strangers in a room right next to them."

Room 402

The door opens and a man dragging a large suitcase trundles in. It's obvious that it's heavy as the man strains to get it up on the bed. He hurriedly turns back to the door, which he closes and locks.

More secrets to keep hidden.

The man is young, probably late twenties but with an early receding hairline. He undoes the zipper that runs around the edge of the suitcase but stops halfway. He shakes his head and nervously does the zip back up, before walking into the bathroom. He comes out with two bath towels, a hand towel and a bath mat, which he tosses onto the bed next to the suitcase. He counts through the pile of towels as if he is hoping to find more. After three tries, he gives up and goes to the door. He unlocks it and opens it just as Pam is about to turn the door handle. They both jump and make small noises.

"I'm sorry, sir," Pam says, laughing. "I didn't realise there was someone in this room. I was just coming back to make sure the room was locked, since I've finished this floor."

"Who are you?" He seems shaken.

"I'm Pam, one the hotel's housekeepers." She holds out her hand, which he doesn't take but still seems pleased to see her.

"I was about to come look for you! Sorry, not you specifically, just someone who can give me more towels."

"Oh, I'm sorry! Did I forget the towels?"

"No!" He says excitedly. "I just need more." There is a pause. "I shower a lot and go through towels quickly."

"Oh, ok." Pam turns to her linen trolley and hands the man three more bath towels. "Is this enough?"

"Could I get another two mats?"

"Certainly," Pam gets two bathmats and turns back to the man. "I will have to make a few extra visits to your room, if that's ok. Otherwise we'll run out of linen for this floor."

"No!" The man has radar-dish eyes. "I mean I sleep, during the day. Naps. I have bad health. It's the same reason I shower a lot."

"Oh, I'm sorry. You can just leave them outside your door."

"Yes! I mean thank you." He's getting very nervous. "Thank you so much." He's forcing an icy smile.

"That's ok. Let me know if you need anything else." She smiles warmly.

"Yes, I will." He awkwardly closes the door with his arms full of towels and mats. He turns around to the bed and pauses, looking at his suitcase. He sighs expectantly then puts the towels on the bed with the others.

Room 403

Svetyana and Ivor are trying to organise everything they need for their first outing in a foreign country. Svetyana is arguing with her son about whether he should bring a backpack or not. Every time their voices get too loud, Svetyana whispers viciously, obviously for both of them to stay quiet. Her son gives up and lies down on his bed with his music blasting from his headphones. Svetyana throws her hands up in the air and speaks quietly to her husband.

It becomes more obvious how much the outside has ruined her.

Even though her son is momentarily deaf by decibels, she is still scared that he will hear her talking about him to Ivor. Secrets born of fear. Not surprisingly, the door to their room is now closed.

Throughout the mother and brother show, Lydia is showing her doll around the room. She goes up to each light switch and performs both the on and off capabilities, before she takes hold of her toy's furry hand and helps it have a try. Her parents don't notice her as she opens the door and walks out of their room, obviously to continue with her toy's guided tour of the hotel.

Room 402

The man is rifling nervously through the bathroom drawers. He opens them and the cupboards repetitively, getting more and more frustrated that whatever it is he is looking for doesn't appear. He gives up and exits the bathroom, then his room, leaving the door open.

The lift's bell's ding can be heard from the hall, as he presses its button. His vacant room is still for a moment before a small, green face looks in from the door. It is followed by a not quite as small girl. Lydia stands in the doorway for a second, and then speaks to her toy. She pauses for a response, nods a reply, and enters the room. She walks around the room, before approaching the suitcase.

She says something to her toy, which responds in what seems to be a hearty nod. Lydia leans over the suitcase until she finds the zipper, which she pulls open, then lifts the lid. Lydia is frozen by what she sees in the suitcase as the man re-enters the room.

He stops.

Lydia turns.

He shuts the door and locks it.

❦

For fifteen years I have made my home here. It was the only space where I could keep the outside where it belonged. I have watched as the dirt, the filth and the disgraces have entered these rooms, but I am safe because I know they will leave. They will return to the outside where they live in the only way they know how — under a roof of lies and secrets and false faces, closed behind seen and unseen doors. Where anyone can be anything and keep it all hidden by the gift of deceit.

This is the only place where I can be alone and protected. Where I no longer live in fear. Because of Pam. She is a light and my ability to see her face every day keeps me alive. She makes me feel safe. She was the only one I had ever seen who holds a torch of purity and magic inside her. Until Lydia.

I will not let this thing, this man, further soil the Earth they tread. Pollute the air they breathe. I owe them that much.

"Who the *fuck* are you?!"

My appearance must scare him. Lydia spins to see me and yet there is no fear in her eyes. She actually smiles. She knew I was here. All along. I hold my arms out and she runs into the circle. My eyes don't leave him. He is frozen. I bend Lydia down so she knows to crawl under the bed, and I take her hands to cover her ears.

He speaks again, "Who the fuck are you?"

I stand and face him. I am the last thing he will ever see.

Room 402

There are two officers and one detective in the room this night. They have attempted to cover what is left of the body with a sheet from the bed. I am glad the man had asked for more towels. It had stopped me from making too much of a mess on the carpet. I didn't want to add to Pams' burden of cleaning.

The wonderful thing about living in a hotel is that no matter how much noise is being made in a room, no one will come and complain if a door is closed. Interrupting privacy and secrecy is more terrifying to a stranger than a person eating their fill of another. Flesh tears from the bone quite easily once the body is relaxed. It must be done soon after death, well before rigor mortis.

Once I have my fill, I return to Lydia. I know she cannot understand my words, so I rely on sound and gesture. As she crawls out from under the bed, I take the hand that isn't holding her toy and cover her eyes with it. I lead her to the door of the room, unlock it, open it, and lightly push her out. I leave the door ajar for anyone passing. Curiosity can sometimes be stronger than fear. The suitcase is also left open.

Lydia makes no mention of me. Neither does Pam, but I know she won't. She has never seen me. Never spoken to me. She thinks secrets can be tolerated. Knows privacy is necessary. It is only when either or both put the ones you love in danger, that a presence needs to be there to protect them. That presence is me.

SONIA MARCON

BIOGRAPHY:

Sonia Marcon began her artistic ventures in creative writing at a young age. Like most children, her interest shifted. It moved from the page to the musical instrument and then in university, the theatrical stage. Now writing has called her back with her first published story, *Phantom Limbs*, which appears in the Ditmar Award winning *Fantastic Wonder Stories* edited by Russell B. Farr.

AFTERWORD:

When the question "what inspired this story" was asked, my only thought of reply was "being in hospital", which is where I end up if the multiple sclerosis I deal with throws a tantrum. I was told to think of seclusion and claustrophobia as a launch base and as yet I haven't experienced anything as secluded or claustrophobic as being in a hospital room tethered to a drip. This, in turn, led me to thinking about what possibly could be *more* secluded and claustrophobic?

My answer, being confined to the crawlspace between the walls of hotel rooms, which is somewhere I have never experienced for any amount of time. So why would someone, or something, choose to live in such a disused area and be surrounded by so many people who are adventuring? Psychosis? Predation? Perversion? I decided on another "P" word; protection. There would be many weird, wonderful but also scary and dangerous people who'd stay in a hotel, so my thought was that there should be a presence protecting those at risk. I have stayed in a good number of hotels and hostels and I think I'd feel comforted to have a guardian angel of sorts watching over me. Or maybe I'm just strange.

THE SUICIDE ROOM

ROOM 415

PAUL KANE

He sat on the bed, staring at the wall in front of him, vaguely hearing the muffled sounds of whoever was on the other side.

Richard Gray blinked and leaned over to open his luggage, his eyes sweeping across the items he'd packed for his stay. Then he reached inside and took out the rope, already conveniently tied in the shape of a noose…

❦

Before he began his research, Richard Gray had no idea there were so many ways to end it all.

But then suicide — from the Latin *suicidium, sui caedere*, to kill oneself — was such a taboo subject. It tended not to crop up in conversation at dinner parties or down the pub (not that he'd know of such things); people didn't stand around the water coolers chatting about the best ways to terminate their existences. It just didn't happen. Suicide was something to be swept under the carpet, something best left to the Samaritans and early morning 'talk shows'.

Online, however, it was another story. As soon as he'd tapped the word into a search engine, thousands of websites had scrolled up before his eyes. Everything from encyclopaedias (more people kill themselves in spring and summer than at any other time of year — the notion that the rates are higher in Winter, and especially at Christmas, was a common misconception) to message boards. Some of the posts on them drew his attention, sad stories of people who'd had enough, the disaffected, the disillusioned, the dissatisfied and, in the end, the disappeared. Entries would tail off, suggesting that the person had simply got on with the task at hand, the unfinished paragraphs merely electronic suicide notes, left behind to show they were once here.

Like him, they'd never really had a voice.

All his life Richard had felt remote, removed from this world. Never right, never fitting in, never belonging...

Broken, wrong.

"What's this in the cubicle? Hey, Liz, it's a little baby..."

"Another one? Jesus, where do they all keep coming from?

"I dunno — but who could just leave their kid like that, abandon them?"

Had he heard the cleaning ladies or was that how he imagined their exchange to be like? As they'd found him, left to be flushed down the public toilet along with the other faeces...

"Stay away from us, stinky! We know where you came from..."

The kids at the orphanage, so cruel, little by little making him into a loner. The words echoed again in his brain. *"Stinky, stinky!"*

And in his working life, as an anonymous maintenance worker in a string of offices — the conversations he'd overheard.

"Don't you think the guy's just a bit... odd. I mean, he never talks to anyone, does he?"

"I don't want him talking to me — gives me the creeps..."

One day he just decided enough was enough. Richard made his choice — and that choice was oblivion.

It was only the method he'd had trouble with. That and the place... He didn't really want to do it at home, his place of retreat... Leaping in front of a train was too public, plus the disruption would have everyone cursing his name (though at least it would finally be on their lips). He didn't own a car or a garage, so carbon monoxide inhalation was out of the question. Nor did he fancy going out to the middle of nowhere to do the deed; all that silence.

Some of the sites he'd visited had recommended hotels, and that seemed to click with him. It was more impersonal, but at the same time not cut off. Yes, that was definitely the way to go. So Richard had toured all the options, looking for the right one — waiting for the right vibe. After all, he was only going to do this once. Finally, he'd come across this place, as day was drifting into night. A transition he could relate to. Richard had looked up from the taxi window and nodded.

After check-in, where he'd gone through the motions of signing the book, knowing that the receptionist's smile was actually saying to him 'Go fuck yourself', he'd carried his luggage up to the first room. But as soon as he stepped through the door, he knew it wasn't right.

"Can I have one facing south," he'd said. They gave it to him, but he wanted to change again. The customer was always right.

On the fourth attempt, he nodded. This was it. Definitely the right room for him.

Richard had laid his case on the bed, and then taken the tour. It was much the same as the other ones he'd looked at, much the same — he guessed — as any other room in any other hotel.

Four walls, thin as paper, a TV that he never intended to turn on let alone watch, a bedside table with the copy of the bible inside the drawer — which he'd turned over — and a bed, the sheets tucked in so tightly they might have been stapled down. It didn't bother Richard; it wasn't as if he'd be getting much sleep that night... well, not in the conventional sense.

Once he was 'settled', he'd sat on the bed next to his case and again turned his attention to the question of 'how'.

This room was on the top floor, just in case. The more serious suicides, he'd read, just flung themselves off buildings, bridges, cliffs — without allowing themselves the time to be talked down. But now he'd paid for the luxury of the room, Richard soon ruled out that notion. To simply jump out of the window would be a waste... Besides, he'd already taken in the drop. Richard had never had much of a head for heights, and the thought of all that time before hitting the ground didn't appeal. They said that everything slowed down as you fell, that your life flashed before your eyes. Whether it was true or not, Richard didn't want to risk it. His life was something he was trying to get away from, not be reminded of.

And what if, by some stroke of luck, the only 'good' luck he'd ever had, he should survive the fall? Would he be destined to spend the rest of his days as some vegetable in a hospital somewhere? Trapped in a body he couldn't escape from?

He'd left the door to the bathroom ajar, after using the toilet earlier; a strangely comforting place for him. As Richard had sat on the loo, he'd gazed at the bath. It wasn't huge, but definitely big enough for a drowning. Then he remembered a piece of advice from one of the sites. It had said simply: 'Water. Don't. It's slow.' Did he have the courage to dunk his head beneath the surface and hold it there? He'd have to fight the automatic survival instinct they said would kick in, the one screaming at him to take a breath as his lungs were exploding. Too much like hard work…

The bath presented another option, though. An old favourite. Lay back and relax as he opened up his veins. He'd brought the razors. Just remember to draw up the forearm, not across the wrists. Given the right mood, it could be an almost spiritual experience, like the Japanese Jigai or Seppuku. Richard shook his head. Too rock star; not his style at all.

How about dropping something electrical *into* the bath, then? This only occurred to him when he was actually in the bathroom, and he realised that he had nothing with a long enough lead to hand — just the TV and a kettle in the room, neither of which would reach. But it did remind him of another technique he'd read about — simply shoving something metal into a plug socket, or smashing the lamps and grabbing hold of the live bits. Quick, effective, but it would probably short out all the electrics in the hotel. And, again, there was always the chance of survival. Did he really want deep burns from 500-1000 volts, ventricular fibrillation from 110-220 volts, and severe neurological damage? Not really. In addition to which, his frying body would set off the smoke detector. That was one of the reasons why he hadn't even contemplated petrol and a match. The last noise he wanted following him into blackness was the annoying *beep-beep-beep* of an alarm.

The noises from the next door room grew louder, laughing. Possibly a couple in the throes of ecstasy? Something Richard had never experienced and never would; that closeness, that—

"He'd better stay away from me, the weirdo."

"Guy gives me the creeps."

Sighing, Richard turned to the case he'd brought. Now he

undid the clasps and opened it, revealing not the usual spread of clothes and toiletries, but another assortment of items altogether.

The noose was the first thing that came to hand, the symbol of all he was contemplating. He took the cord, pulling it to test its strength. Not too thin or too weak, he'd bought it with one task in mind. Looking around the room again, however, he couldn't see any good places from which to swing. Over a door, perhaps, with the rope tied to the handle and him standing on a chair. But what if the rope should slide off the top? The only thing hurt would be his pride.

How about tying the rope to the door and just yanking, like pulling a tooth? Falling forwards with the rope tight would do it... unless his knees buckled and he toppled sideways. Richard tossed down the noose in dismay. This was much more difficult than he'd thought.

He reached into the case again and took out the container full of pills. It rattled like a small set of maracas. Inside were various different kinds of medications: sleeping tablets, paracetamol, aspirins... and some of the more exotic kind. A handful of those washed down with the bottle of vodka — also in the case — would do the trick, definitely.

His eyes were drawn to the array of plastic bags he'd stuffed inside the case. Richard examined each in turn, picking up first one, then another, trying to choose which would be best for placing over his head and cutting off his supply of oxygen. Some had handles he could tie tightly, so that even if he wanted to undo the knot he wouldn't be able to. A couple had drawstrings to make it even easier. Neither of which would stop him ripping open the plastic if he got into a panic.

Richard rummaged through his belongings once more, shifting the bags to one side and revealing the variety of knives he'd gathered. They glinted in the light from the lamp as he pulled them out one by one, all different shapes and sizes. Each had its own purpose: scalpel-like for slicing the jugular or the corroded artery; serrated, hunting blades for shoving into his internal organs and causing the maximum damage; needle-thin for puncturing the eye and ramming into the brain, or even up the nose. Silently, Richard deliberated their merits and drawbacks…

Before turning to the case and bringing out the last of the objects.

He held the weapon carefully in his hands. There were more muffled sounds from the adjoining room; he ignored them. The gun had its safety catch on, but it was already loaded and, as such, demanded he handle it delicately. Richard didn't want it to go off accidentally, injuring him but not finishing the job. This was the ultimate way: the one all the 'experts' had recommended. Up against the temple, pull the trigger. *Blam!* Over in an instant. All it would take was a little courage of his behalf. Richard experimentally brought up the barrel and rested the cold metal against his forehead. He placed his thumb against the trigger, just to see what it felt like. He breathed in and out quickly, his adrenalin pumping.

Taking the pistol away, he lifted his chin and thrust the barrel into the fleshy bit beneath. Richard closed his eyes, his breathing even quicker.

This is what it will be like, just before the end? Will you be able to pull the trigger? Can you do it?

His eyes still closed, he opened his mouth and wrapped his lips around the barrel, angling it so that the bullet would shoot up through the roof and into his skull.

If you're going to do it, you might as well get on with it… Stop dithering about what to do and just slip off the safety, pull the trigger. Then it'll all be over…

With his thumb, Richard unlocked the safety catch. He was breathing hard through his nose, so hard the wind made it whistle. Richard was conscious of his finger on the trigger of the gun. It was trembling; in fact his whole hand was shaking. Just a little more pressure was all it would take, just a little more…

Bang, bang, bang!

The knocks were sharp and hard, almost causing Richard to inadvertently pull the trigger. But he had enough sense to realise that his aim would be completely off if he did: he'd just end up shooting a bloody big hole through his cheek.

Richard withdrew the pistol from his mouth.

"Sir, sir, are you there?" A woman's voice, hushed and with a trace of an accent… Russian? Polish maybe.

He rose, pressing his face up against the door, looking through the peephole. It threw back a distorted image of a female member of staff, with short, blonde hair, wearing the hideous standardised uniform of the hotel.

"Sir… Please!" She knocked on the door again, making him jump.

Richard swallowed dryly, his voice cracking as he said, "Go away; I'm busy." A few more seconds, just a few more then this would all have been over.

"Sir… Mr Gray, I have an urgent message for you."

A message? Richard frowned. Impossible. No one knew even he was here, let alone cared.

"There must be some sort of mistake."

He watched through the peephole as she shook her head. "No mistake."

"Who's it from?" he asked, his curiosity piqued.

"I am to give to you in person."

Richard let his head rest on the door for a second, before undoing the latch with his free hand, opening up. The woman was virtually on the threshold of the door, and she looked directly at him with the bluest eyes he'd ever seen.

"Alright…"

She opened her mouth to speak, then looked over his shoulder into the room beyond. Richard realised at the last minute, when he saw the expression on her face, that she'd seen the selection of knives on the bed.

Idiot! She probably thinks you're a serial killer or something! Now she'll get the police involved and they'll lock you up, either in jail or…somewhere else, somewhere they can keep an eye on you and make sure that you never get a chance to do this again… Shit!

She looked like she was about to scream, so instinctively he showed her the gun he was still holding. "Please don't," he warned her. "Come in… close the door." He backed off and watched as she entered, shutting the door behind her.

Richard waved her into the centre of the room, and she shifted sideways like a crab, holding her hands in the air.

"There's… there's no need for that," he assured her. "I'm not going to hurt you. Okay?"

She shook her head. He didn't know whether she hadn't fully understood or just didn't believe him.

"I'm not going to hurt *anyone*." Richard paused, realising that wasn't strictly the truth but not knowing how he could explain himself.

"I-I know." Her voice was even more timid now, the accent more pronounced.

Richard frowned again. Had he really been that convincing? "I'm really not a bad person," he went on, attempting to bolster his argument.

She nodded. Was she agreeing with him or arguing that he was?

"I wish you hadn't seen all this stuff. I didn't want an audience."

This was the most conversation he'd ever had with a woman in his life, and it was at gunpoint, probably the only way one would stand and listen to him. But this wasn't helping. He had to figure out a way of dealing with the situation. Tie her up until he'd completed his task? He had plenty of rope… But could he just carry on knowing she was in here with him? Even putting her in the bathroom wouldn't do any good; he'd still know she was there.

You don't have long, he told himself, *she'll be missed soon; they'll send people to look for her, to find out where she is. She only came up to deliver the…*

"You never said who it was from," Richard blurted out, "the message."

"No…No, I did not," she admitted.

"Alright, so…"

She looked down then back up at him. The noises from the adjourning rooms were increasing. Voices, either from the TV or people arguing, were being raised.

"This will sound strange to you, but when I said before that I know… I meant I know why you come here, what you come here for. I knew even before.. " The blonde woman pointed to the knives on the bed, the gun in his hand.

"How could you?"

"It is the room," she explained. "You find it, or it finds you. I am not sure exactly how it works. But the people who stay in it only have one thought on their minds."

Richard blinked. "What are you telling me?"

"Guests who use this room, they wish to hurt themselves. Are you telling me you do not?"

He understood this kind of thing happened occasionally; that's what had given him the idea in the first place. But in the *same* hotel, in the *same* room? "There... there have been others? Here?"

The woman nodded.

"How many?"

"Enough," she replied, "over the years. But not enough to draw attention. The people who come here are not missed. *You* will not be missed," she added.

That was true, but it hurt to hear it out loud — especially coming from her. "You tricked me to get inside. Why?"

The woman drew closer, taking a couple of steps towards him. "You have not fully made up your mind; there is still hope."

Richard almost spat out the laugh. "Hope? You've got to be kidding me. Hope's the last thing I have."

"Then why answer the door to me? Why did you think the message was for you? That someone would be trying to reach you, somewhere... even though you knew it could not be."

"I... I don't know..." Richard was lowering the gun. "Who are you? What are you really doing here?"

"I am Nissa." She stated her name like it would explain everything.

"That doesn't answer my question."

"It answers the first one." She attempted a weak smile but it just didn't work. "I am someone who understands the pain you must be feeling. You think that nothing matters. That nothing you do, day after day, is of any consequence."

Richard's mouth hung open. "You can't know, nobody does. *Nobody* cares!"

"Not true." Her voice was stronger now. "More care than you realise… Listen, Richard. Listen to them."

The noise from the rooms on either side was escalating, so loud now it would surely bring complaints from the other guests. However, the closer Richard concentrated on them, the more he realised the truth; the voices were not getting louder at all, there were just more of them. Layers upon layers, coming from inside the room *itself*. He fell to his knees, the gun toppling from his grasp onto the floor in front of him.

"Listen," Nissa encouraged him. "Hear them."

He had no option, because they were speaking directly to him, *at* him. But who did they belong to? Who were they?

"It is what you will become," Nissa explained, breaking through the cacophony, answering his unspoken question, "if you go through with your intent." Her accent wasn't just foreign now, he realised: it sounded warped, like a tape running too slowly then too quickly.

The hotel room was suddenly much smaller than it had been a few moments ago, the sound somehow shrinking its size.

"Who are you?" screamed Richard, hands clasped against the side of his head. *"What* are you?"

"You have so much to live for. That was the message I brought."

In spite of what was going on, Richard snorted. "If you're going to show me what would have happened if I'd never existed, don't bother. There's no point. I can't help you get your wings."

Now it was Nissa's turn to laugh. "You really do not understand, do you? I was drawn to you, just as you were drawn to this room. But it does not have you yet. Listen, Richard Gray, listen to their stories…"

Like those on the message boards, the voices were desperate to tell him their tales, separating and becoming plainer. They painted their words on his mind's eye, forcing him not only to hear them, but to see as well. This wasn't possible, he told himself; Richard knew that he shouldn't be witnessing this — yet he was.

One thing was for sure: if the way he'd been considering his suicide had been clinical, detached, then *their* stories brought home the reality of it to him.

Richard saw an overweight man in his forties take a razor to his throat, the warm redness spraying everywhere as the man staggered about the room. He saw a girl who couldn't have been more than eighteen, shooting up with a needle, her eyes rolling back in her head as she collapsed over the bed. He saw a man wearing spectacles hang himself using the light fitting, something Richard hadn't even thought of; pictured the jerking body, the tongue and spittle flying from the man's mouth until he was dead. He saw an old man garrotting himself, his tongue flopping out like a slug. Richard saw drownings and wrist-slittings in the bath and over the sink, not to mention swan dives from the window.

But for every method Richard had contemplated, there were others — some so creative they were bordering on the artistic. One person had brought dozens of bees into the room and released them, so that they stung him to death: his body a mass of lumpen and swollen flesh by the time they were finished. Another had run at the wall, two, three times, until he could do so no more — until his skull was mashed in. Someone else had poured acid all over themselves, biting down hard on a piece of wood as the liquid melted flesh and bone. Yet another had swallowed bleach, then spent agonising, rasping hours dying on the floor of the room; burning from the inside out.

The reasons accompanied them, too: bankruptcy; loss of husbands, wives, offspring…homes; blackmail; discovered affairs; guilt; boredom; pacts. Every possible explanation and then some.

Richard finally began crying when he heard the story of the family who'd checked into the room, the mother and father killing their children first before turning on each other, the world and all its evils too much for them to face. It was then that he realised it hadn't been laughing he'd heard earlier at all; rather it had been the screams of the damned.

"They thought as you did…once." It was Nissa's distinctive voice, but from so far away. "They thought that oblivion was better than going on. But they soon learned. There *is* no oblivion. *No* release. Only this room."

"Enough…Please! I've heard enough."

She was a blur through watery eyes, a shape walking towards him. "No Heaven. No Hell. Somewhere in-between. Trapped with their pain."

"How?" he asked her one last time. "How do you know all this? How *could* you."

The voices quietened. Dying down now that they'd had their say, allowing Nissa to bend and whisper in his ear. Richard listened to her story, finally: someone who'd seen her parents shot and killed at an early age, the victims of a war no-one had heard of or cared about; an immigrant who'd sought a better life in another country, only to find a nightmare waiting for her; a woman who'd been hired out to clients in this very hotel by the men who had brought her across; 'paying them back' they'd called it.

Richard blinked. Nissa's form had changed. She was completely naked, her skin a cold white, lips as blue as her eyes — which now stood out all the more. She was one of their number; a true definition of a suicide blonde. And she was as close to an angel as anything he'd ever seen.

"I sought to save you from this fate. At last, someone who was not sure, someone who might be convinced... I knew you don't really want to die, not deep down. I was able to connect with you, appear to you. Show you this is not the way."

The tears rolled down Richard's eyes. How could he tell her? That no, he hadn't been completely convinced. There had been the tiniest of doubts in his mind. Until she'd come along: the one person, it appeared, who had ever understood him, ever really cared what happened to him, from the cradle to...

Nissa had been, still was, like him: broken, wrong.

They were destined to be together.

Could he bear to lose that connection now? Get up and walk out of that door, never to return again, never to see Nissa again. Wouldn't that make going on *even more* difficult? God in Heaven, whatever her intentions, all she had done was made the choice that much clearer for him.

And show him the way.

Richard looked down at the abandoned gun, looked over at the things he'd brought with him. None of them had been necessary at all. To end your life all you really had to do was relinquish your hold on it, just as she'd done. Be so definite in your purpose. Let the final breaths escape from your body, become aware of what you are and what you don't want to be any more:

Alive.

"Wait," shouted Nissa. "Richard. What are you doing?

What he had to, in order to remain here. In Suicide Room. With Nissa, with the other lost souls. Bound to it, neither one thing nor the other.

"Richard…No, don't-"

He smiled.

Yes, there would be pain, there would be suffering; a reliving of death. But he'd pay the price gladly.

Richard Gray fell over sideways on the floor of the room, not breathing, his eyes staring upwards at Nissa — glazed over in death. But in those final moments as he turned his back on the living world to join her, he realised: there never had been any way to end it all, not really.

At least he would not be alone any more. He was with his own kind. Now Richard belonged, now he fitted in. Always would.

And, in the months — the years — to come, when more victims would be drawn to this place, just as he had been, Richard could at last tell his tale. Not hoping to stop them, as Nissa had attempted, but just to have a captive audience.

One among many, but a voice nonetheless. A voice forever remote…

Forever removed from this world.

PAUL KANE

BIOGRAPHY:

Paul Kane has been writing professionally for twelve years. His genre journalism has appeared in such magazines as *The Dark Side, Death Ray, Fangoria, SFX, Dreamwatch* and *Rue Morgue*, and his first non-fiction book was the critically acclaimed *The Hellraiser Films and Their Legacy*, introduced by Doug 'Pinhead' Bradley.

His short stories have appeared in many magazines and anthologies on both sides of the Atlantic, in all kinds of formats (as well as being broadcast on BBC Radio 2), and have been collected in *Alone (In the Dark)*, *Touching the Flame* and *FunnyBones*. His novella *Signs of Life* reached the shortlist of the British Fantasy Awards 2006 and *The Lazarus Condition* was introduced by Mick Garris, creator of *Masters of Horror*.

His first mass market novel is *Arrowhead*, a post-apocalyptic reworking of the Robin Hood myth published by Abaddon as part of their Afterblight series. In his capacity as Special Publications Editor of the British Fantasy Society he worked with and edited authors like Brian Aldiss, Ramsey Campbell, Muriel Gray, Graham Masterton, Robert Silverberg and many more.

In 2008 his zombie story *Dead Time* was turned into an episode of the Lionsgate/NBC TV series Fear Itself, adapted by Steve Niles (*30 Days of Night*) and directed by Darren Lynn Bousman (*SAW II-IV*) with FX from Oscar-winners KNB.

Paul's website, which has featured guest writers such as Stephen King, Clive Barker and Neil Gaiman, can be found at www.shadow-writer.co.uk He currently lives in Derbyshire, UK, with his wife — the author Marie O'Regan — his family, and a black cat called Mina.

AFTERWORD:

I've been wanting to write a story about a hotel room and suicide ever since a friend of mine mentioned that there were sites on the net which dealt with the best ways to top yourself, and the best locations (before you ask, yes, that friend is still very much with us — it was just morbid curiosity). As it says in the story, an anonymous hotel room is still a favourite place to do the deed, so when I read the guidelines for *Voices* the two just sort of married together really. I felt it was important to include some aspect of the title in my story, so that's when I decided to give the Suicides in this particular tale their own, individual voices; after all, no-one listened to them in life

THE MAN WHO WASN'T THERE

ROOM 428

RODNEY J. SMITH

A sh pushed the door open with one arm and hurled his suitcase inside with the other. Every muscle in his body was adding its voice to a mutiny. His mind was just as fed up.

He'd spent more than a day's worth of flying, every airport another agonising wait in line after line, as each hour of his connection time ticked by on overhead clocks. It was all timed perfectly to deny him any chance of breakfast but leave him just enough seconds to make it to the next gate for final boarding call -
— if he ran the whole way.

To finish the whole affair in style, the shuttle had dropped him at his hotel precisely thirteen minutes after the bar had closed.

He was getting sick of living like this.

His stomach twisted and his fingers trembled as his hungry body started dipping into its sugar reserves.

In less than five hours, he'd be dragging himself back out of bed to meet another roomful of arseholes who didn't care who he was.

In fairness, the opposite was just as true. Their names and faces would evaporate as quickly as their superficial pleasantries in the hours between that conference and the next one.

Another city, another circle of laptops in a meeting room not unlike the last; another cloud of coffee-breath smelling decidedly worse than the cup it came from; another set of teasingly smooth legs squeezed into a business skirt, the face above them a pretty one if it was one of the better mornings; another day in a life that denied him everything but refused to let him go.

This room was no different to any other he'd passed through as another anonymous suit. A tiny kitchen with an attached bathroom greeted him just beyond the door; beyond those, a combined living and sleeping area, where his deluxe queen bed was ready and turned down. The AC was keeping the temperature just right. Easy-listening tunes drifted softly from a bedside radio. As a younger man, these carefully configured rooms did the trick in replicating that home-away-from-home feeling. Nowadays, he saw past the lie; the emptiness that lay beneath the welcoming surface only reminded him how homeless he truly was.

It couldn't have been more than a few minutes since his head had hit the pillow, but the alarm shrieking beside him was adamant that the time for rest had passed.

He hit it harder than he needed to.

He was reluctant to pull his clothes on after the shower. These were the things that bound him, set him to work in his prison. The stiff shoes worked to cripple him, their campaign to callous his feet realizing its triumph as the years passed. The tie around his neck was a noose that wasn't quite tight enough to finish the job.

It choked him slowly instead.

The strangest thing occurred as he shaved. Halfway through his right cheek, he met a man who wasn't there.

The fact alone was disturbing enough. And discourse with the man was certainly not a conversation in the traditional sense. Yet there he was -- rather, there the definite *lack* of a man was.

The whole thing was a paradox, yet Ash found he accepted the situation rather quickly. In fact, he was quite open to the notion, even envious of the man. For he too, wished he wasn't there.

You don't have to be, the man told him.

If only it were that simple. If only he wasn't here in this city at all.

You can leave it all.

That'd be great, to just get up and go. But he was trapped. There was a seat in the business centre downstairs with his name on it. Then there were all those cell phones that could track him down no matter where he hid. There were pagers, email. They didn't care about him, but they'd sure get a lot more interested if he held up a meeting. Then it'd be even worse, having to explain why he'd never shown up in the first place.

But that's only if you're somewhere to be found. If you're nowhere...

Nowhere at all? But how?

Give up your name.

Ash laughed; a strained, rough sound he didn't much care for. He didn't like being connected to it. He didn't want it belonging to him.

What's so funny?

If only it were that easy: just change your name, disappear. But you still had to pay your bills, register your car; there'd always be a record with your new name. People could find you. There was always a paper trail.

You don't change your label. You leave it. You leave.

What's the difference?

Your thinking is still rooted in the physical. If you're no longer here, you can't be touched by anything.

What, like disappear, literally? Be a ghost?

No. Just be gone.

Ash spied a streak of blood sliding its way to his collar. The razor was clasped in a white-knuckled fist. Its blade was pressed into his cheek. He dropped it in the basin and reached for a tissue.

What did that mean, 'gone'? Was that even possible? It's not like this man was gone, if he could talk to him.

And yet, there's no one here.

Ash stared at the sunken, tired eyes of the man in the mirror. A little spark ignited in his chest, a growing excitement. He laughed again, genuinely this time, though he still didn't like the sound. The point, however, could evoke no other response. It was so obvious, so simple, it bordered on ludicrous.

To just not be here. But how?

Discard the name that keeps you. Free yourself of its designation. Your connection to it ties you to that nametag...to that chair downstairs...to your life.

Ash fingered the plastic tag pinned to his tie. 'HI! I'm ASH', it declared to the bathroom mirror. He didn't want to be here. He didn't want to be Ash.

His fingers trembled at the prospect. He pulled it free.

But what now?

Close a door on it. Separate yourself from it.

Ash headed for the closet. Each carpeted step felt like a thunderous stomp in an empty cavern. The nametag stuck to his sweaty palm, growing heavier with each step as the weight of its impending release settled in his chest.

He opened the closet, the room's dull lighting slicing the darkness within. He took a deep breath and tossed the nametag inside.

Close the door on it. Break the connection.

His fingers trembled on the handle. He had the door halfway closed when he suddenly wasn't so sure.

What would it be like, when he was gone? Would it hurt?

There will be no pain. There will be nothing to feel.

There was comfort in the thought, but also a cold sense of loss. He had to have it back in his hand. He had to hold onto his name just a little longer.

He dropped to his knees in the closet and found the nametag, clutching it to his breast. He was crying before he could do anything about it, uncontrollable sobs that rocked him as he huddled in the shadow with his name.

What are you crying for?

My life.

A life that keeps you trapped in misery.

What does it matter if I want to stay?

It only matters to you. You're the only one here.

Ash saw the truth of this again, and it made him rethink what he was defending — and who he was arguing with.

His life *was* a misery. The random moments of pleasure he dared to hope for would not outweigh that, even if they all came true.

The only things guaranteed on this march were more strangers, more hotel rooms, more days blurring into night in a never ending carousel of sleep deprivation.

And in the end, he would be too old to do anything about it. And then he would die.

But if he wasn't here, he wouldn't have to face that drawn-out parade of decay.

If he was gone,

If he *wasn't here,*

There'd be nothing for the world to touch.

Ash turned the nametag over in his fingers a few times, trying to suppress a smile as he bid insincere farewells. The closer he came to standing up, the further removed from the thing in his hands, and what it represented, he became.

By the time he unfolded his left leg to rise, it was already something he no longer considered his own. It was just a thing, attached to another thing he'd also stopped identifying as something he owned.

There would be nothing to own in a matter of seconds. There would be no-one here responsible for any of it.

He placed the nametag in the centre of the closet and stared at it one last time from the doorway.

Then he closed the door, and he was gone.

RODNEY J. SMITH

BIOGRAPHY:

Rodney J. Smith is originally from Melbourne, Australia. Most of his stories are dark or surreal, filled with people and places that aren't quite right. For more of his work, visit www.rodneyjsmith.com

AFTERWORD:

The Man Who Wasn't There was inspired by a creepy little rhyme my mother taught me when I was a boy, which she herself heard as a child. I've since learned it came from a song in a 1910 play called *The Psyco-ed.*

Voices offered the perfect location in which to set the story — as well as a deadline to make me actually write it.

REMAINDERS

2008

ROBERT HOOD

Floor 4.

What with the elevator being out of order, and carrying all that luggage she'd brought, Tara found that the prospect of having the best view of the city had lost its appeal. It wasn't a long climb to get to the top but she was tired and grumpy, and had wanted this stay to be comfortable. Pessimistically she saw the four flights of stairs as a premonition of discomfort to come.

What was worse in her mind was the fact that there had been nobody in the lobby to help her — nobody willing to help anyway. She'd asked the anaemic-looking specimen behind the registration desk, but the woman had just growled, "Can't help, love. I'm on the desk."

"Fine, but surely there's someone else."

"All busy, love. You can leave the bags if you like. I'll get the porter to bring them up when he's got a moment."

Tara didn't trust the woman or the suspicious-looking character hunkered down behind a newspaper in the far corner of the lobby. She suspected her bags would go missing. So she'd picked them up and headed for the stairs. They were inordinately heavy. Why had she brought so much?

At first the door had refused to open; she had to put down the bags again and wrestle with the fucking doorhandle. Didn't they want her to stay at this place? It was certainly no way to run a business.

Not that it was much of a business. The hotel had been built early last century and though the automatic lift, albeit non-functional, and advertised TV and internet access indicated that upgrades had happened since then, it was in these latter days looking the worse for wear. There were so few people around. This was prime tourist season, yet Tara herself and the man in the lobby with the newspaper were the only non-staffers she'd seen. At this time of the day there should have been people leaving, people arriving. There should have been a buzz happening in the lobby. But it had echoed hollowly and smelt of abandonment. Hotel bookings were so difficult right now in this part of town, not even the place's two-star rating could account for the silence.

The stairwell, too, smelt of decay. Tara paused at the first floor landing to catch her breath. Out of curiosity and thinking that filling her lungs with cleaner air might be a good idea, she tried the door with the huge faded "1" stamped on it. It wouldn't budge. That couldn't be right. With the lift down, shouldn't all the access doors be unlocked?

She jerked away from the door as something thudded against it, so hard she felt it shudder. "Is someone there?" she called. After waiting through a few moments of silence, she leaned in and gently tapped on the peeling surface. "Hello?"

No one answered, but Tara could feel a presence — someone waiting, listening. Were they saying something? She put her ear to the door. The wood was surprisingly warm. For a moment she heard nothing then a low growl reached her, sending ice into her stomach. Something scratched across the other side of the barrier.

She stood away from it, frowning. Probably some kid mucking around. But whatever it was, she didn't intend to stay and find out. Grabbing her luggage, she kept going upward.

The impulse to book into this place had come out of nowhere. It had started when she received an email message — spam, no doubt, an ad for the hotel — and while she normally trashed unsolicited mail instantly, this time a deeply felt impulse had stopped her. Her firewall was up-to-date, featuring all the latest virus-detecting software, so it was unlikely to be a threat to her hard-drive. Instead of hitting the "DELETE" key, she'd clicked on the accompanying link. It had taken her to a webpage that had made the hotel seem intriguing. Perhaps it was a sign, she'd thought, a sign that I need a holiday.

The Second Floor landing was as uninviting as the First, the dull lights flickering so that patches of darkness seemed to move around her. But Tara was a bit breathless now, so she stopped for a rest anyway. Curious to know whether all the doors were locked, she tried the handle. It wouldn't move. Annoyed, she slammed her palm against it, causing an echo that reverberated harshly and faded downward into whatever basement area was situated far below. As the sound died, she thought she heard someone scream. Faint, but definitely a scream. It had come from the other side of the door to Floor 2.

She tried the handle again, more urgently this time, but still without result. "Hello? Is anyone in there?" she yelled. "Hello? Do you need help?"

The determined silence made her feel like a nervous fool. Once more she grabbed her bags and headed upward.

She had to admit that there had been aspects to the hotel that worried her, or rather that should have worried her had she not instead allowed them to intrigue her. A Google search on the name of the place brought up few positive testimonials, but did offer tales of death and even whispers of ghostly hauntings. Naturally Tara dismissed the latter as superstition harnessed in the cause of publicity. The bizarre accidental deaths and even more bizarre murders simply gave the hotel an exotic ambiance.

The final piece fell into place when she stumbled upon mention of a man named Brighton Jones, who had died horribly as a result of an ill-defined elevator accident in the hotel at the beginning of last century. "Jones" was of course one of the single most common names on the face of the planet, but "Brighton Jones"? How many of those could there be? Well, as it turned out, quite a few; one was a high-powered financial advisor. But it didn't take her long to eliminate the living Brighton Joneses and to finally determine that the one who'd died in the hotel's elevator in 1928 was, in all probability, her great-great grandfather. In fact, as Tara's parents and their siblings were all dead, Tara was possibly Brighton Jones' only surviving descendent.

The idea had caught her imagination — "sparked some blood bonding", as one of her friends had put it — and she'd booked a room on the top floor of the hotel after very little toing and froing. Why the top floor? She had no idea. At the time the management had told her that that was where the only free rooms were available — clearly a lie. Anyway, they'd said, there was a good view of the city from Room 413.

Sure enough when she reached the landing of the Third Floor, Tara found that the door into the hotel proper was locked. She was going to be very pissed off if, when she got to the top, the Floor 4 entry was locked as well. It wasn't looking hopeful. She sighed and gathered her strength to go on.

But someone was sobbing. She heard the sound just as she got her bags properly balanced for the final climb. She paused, considering if it was worth investigating, given her track record so far. As she made up her mind to call out, just in case someone needed help, the surface of the entry door began to bulge inward. She sucked in her breath — and the lights in the stairwell went out with a loud pop. That was when her rapidly adjusting eyes made out the vague shape of a figure looking at her in the greyness of the gloomy space.

"Who are you?" she said, backing up the stairs.

"I'm sorry. I didn't mean to scare you." The voice was low and sad, sliding into her mind like a half-heard whisper.

"Was that you crying?" Tara asked impulsively. "On the Third Floor?"

"Someone else," the man said. *"I need your help."*

"Help?"

"To get to the Fourth Floor. It keeps me away."

"I don't know what you're talking about." Tara glanced nervously past the man, down the stairwell. "I could fetch the manager."

"I never reached the top. Now it prevents me because there I am free. Free to act. But your blood can carry me."

"My–"

"I called you and you came."

"Who are you?"

"You carry the blood I no longer have."

Realisation sparked in Tara's mind. As absurd as it might have seemed mere minutes before, it revealed itself to her as a certainty now. She held out her hand and the spectre grasped it. She had anticipated a cold, hard grip, but his fingers seemed to meld with hers. In a moment the world darkened into a blind, senseless abyss; Tara felt nowhere, felt nothing. She floated.

A voice said, *"Let me go now."*

She was standing a few metres from the stairwell door on Floor 4, hands flat against the wall. Her head felt numb, the world fractured around her and trying to draw itself back together.

As the disorientation dissipated, Tara realised she was near a window. She looked out through the dusty glass, but all she could see was swirling smoke. "This is the best view of the city?" she muttered.

"Did you bring what I asked?"

The man's form swept out from the substance of the wall, where he had taken refuge, and stood before her. It hadn't been a dream then.

"Bring what you asked?" she said. "I don't know. Did you ask me to bring something?"

"Open the bag." He pointed at the larger of her two travel bags.

"It's just –"

"Please. Open it."

She did. Inside was what looked like plastic bottles full of a metallic yellow liquid. She slammed the lid shut.

"That's not mine!"

"You should go," the man said.

Tara looked in his eyes. They were black and empty, but something burned far down in the depths of them. And it was drawing closer.

"Go while you can," he added. *"A few more must die and it will be over."*

"What are you going to do?"

Now his eyes flared. *"Go! Please!"*

She ran to the stairwell and plunged into its darkness. Behind her the flames were spreading quickly.

Now it was the hotel's turn to scream.

EPILOGUE

The crumbling ruins of the building had been partially cleared away. Here and there, ash still moved in tiny scurrying ripples across burnt beams of wood and fallen masonry. Almost like something there is alive, thought Ruben Brookshire.

"We should have it cleared by the end of the week," a gruff voice said.

"Really?" Ruben glanced around at the workman. He was bulky and sun-hardened but his eyes were gentle. "What happens then?"

The man shrugged, his shoulders moving like tectonic plates. "You the owner?"

"Me? No. I'm a journalist. I read about the disaster in the paper. I was curious, that's all."

"Didn't cover it?"

"I don't do news. I'm a feature writer — write about..." He smiled weakly. "Haunted houses. Weird shit."

"Yeah? They useta say this place was haunted, you know?"

Ruben nodded. "That's why I was interested. I always meant to investigate the place. I'll never know now, I guess."

"You believe in that shit?"

Ruben shrugged. "Not really. Makes good copy though."

The workman nodded. "Bloody shame. It was an old building, you know? One of those fancy places from way back. Prob'ly had a ton of history attached to it. And lotsa ghosts."

Ruben gazed out over the rubble. "They have any idea what happened yet?"

"Probably someone fell asleep in bed with a fag." The man pointed at the ruins like an accuser. "Safety measures were ratshit. Take it from me, the place was an accident waitin' to happen."

"Everyone died then?"

"Some woman got out. No one else though. They found one bloke down the back. He was singed and woulda made it, but a hunk of masonry fell on him. Crushed his back. Snuffed him like that." He snapped his fingers. "They reckon he was the porter."

"Bad luck, eh?"

"Talkin' of weird shit..." A conspiratorial look came over the workman's features. "Some reckon he'd worked in the hotel for like... well, as long as anyone can remember. But the cops say he was only 35 or somethin'."

"Guess it wasn't the same man then."

"Guess not."

Silence fell between them. Finally the workman excused himself, mumbled that it was nice talking to Ruben and wandered off. Ruben kept staring across the ruins.

A movement caught his attention, something larger than the shifting ash. He turned. In the shadows of a collapsed wall he thought he could see a human-like shape, dim and unlit, as though twilight had fallen in that spot alone. Ruben stared at it, trying to focus. A chill eased into his spine and he shivered. A wind? No, the shape was looking straight at him — he was convinced of it. He took a step or two in the opposite direction.

Flames flared up around the figure and Ruben could see it clearly for one incandescent moment. A man, average build, wearing a dull grey suit. Then the flame was gone and so was the man.

What was it?

"Almost like something there is alive," Ruben whispered into the breeze.

ROBERT HOOD

BIOGRAPHY:

Robert Hood once stayed in a hotel room where, through a long lonely night, he was forced to listen to the spectral cries of the forlorn and the eternally damned. Of course the fact that the hotel was situated in the CBD of Australia's national capital, Canberra, and that the ghosts wailing in the night were public servants celebrating the end of the working week, only made it scarier. When not contemplating the end of sanity as we know it, Hood writes the sort of stories that make his aging mother wonder what she did wrong. Over 160 of them have appeared in print to date, many collected into books. *Creeping in Reptile Flesh* (Altair Australia Books, 2008) is the latest. For more, visit his website at roberthood.net.

AFTERWORD:

When the editors of *Voices* asked if I would write short pieces to introduce each section of the thematic anthology, I said yes with some enthusiasm. Short short stories (or "flash fiction" as they are often called) are difficult and brevity is not something that comes naturally to me. But lately I've become attracted to the idea of writing a series of separate short short stories that form a sequence that has some sort of unity in itself. Short and long all in the one package! I had recently done it in the story "Moments of Dying" (*Black* magazine, Issue 1, July 2008). There the sequence is held together not by characters or a single narrative thread, but through thematic resonance.

With *Voices*, I tried to produce six separate stories that were held together by a single character, but one that only featured peripherally in all but the first and penultimate stories. In the remainder he would play a role that would only become entirely clear in retrospect — thus giving the whole a sort of hidden narrative structure as well.

Other restrictions more directly related to the anthology were governed by the section titles and the fact that the stories would be set not in the hotel's rooms but in the corridors on each floor. The progression from lobby to Floor 4 would also help give the sequence a developmental unity.

But why the 20 year gaps, I hear you ask?

Again there was a structural benefit, but mostly I thought it would be fun to ring subtle changes in the building and the individual characters that reflected the various periods. In the end of course, the separate stories weren't always as short as I anticipated..

176

ABOUT THE EDITORS

MARK S. DENIZ

Mark S. Deniz lives in Norrköping, on the south east coast of Sweden, with his wife Etina, and their son Maddoc.

A novelist and short fiction writer, Mark recently turned his hand to screenwriting for a short film *Silverudden*, which was screened at festivals worldwide in 2007. His published short stories (under the nom-de-plume Sin Deniz) can be found in the Big Finish anthologies: *A Life Worth Living, Something Changed,* and Collected Works. He also features in *FlashSpec: Volume Two,* and will appear in the forthcoming *Black Box* anthology and *Doorways Magazine,* both scheduled for a 2008 release.

After a successful year at Eneit Press, Mark has started his own company, Morrígan Books, closely followed by its imprint Gilgamesh Press, which is to focus on Assyrian topics. More can be found regarding Mark on his Live Journal account: http://mark.deniz.livejournal.com.

AMANDA PILLAR

Amanda Pillar is a speculative fiction author and editor who lives in Victoria, Australia, with her only child, a Burmese cat.

Amanda has six short stories in print, with three more awaiting publication. She is also the co-editor of the post-apocalyptic anthology, *Grants Pass* and the speculative short story collection, The *Phantom Queen Awakes,* both of which are to be published by Morrígan Books.

In her free time, she plans on becoming the next Indiana Jones.

Read about her adventures at http://amandapillar.livejournal.com or by visiting her website: www.amandapillar.com.

ABOUT THE COVER ARTIST

REECE NOTLEY

I don't have a bio. I just lived. I never took notes! NO ONE TOLD ME I HAD TO TAKE FRICKING NOTES!

Sheesh.